Here's what critics are saying about
Leslie Langtry's books:

"I laughed so hard I cried on multiple occasions while reading MARSHMALLOW S'MORE MURDER! Girl Scouts, the CIA, and the Yakuza... what could possibly go wrong?"
—Fresh Fiction

"Darkly funny and wildly over the top, this mystery answers the burning question, 'Do assassin skills and Girl Scout merit badges mix…' one truly original and wacky novel!"
—RT BOOK REVIEWS

"Those who like dark humor will enjoy a look into the deadliest female assassin and PTA mom's life."
—Parkersburg News

"Mixing a deadly sense of humor and plenty of sexy sizzle, Leslie Langtry creates a brilliantly original, laughter-rich mix of contemporary romance and suspense in *'Scuse Me While I Kill This Guy.*"
—Chicago Tribune

"The beleaguered soccer mom assassin concept is a winner, and Langtry gets the fun started from page one with a myriad of clever details."
—Publisher's Weekly

BOOKS BY LESLIE LANGTRY

Merry Wrath Mysteries:
Merit Badge Murder
Mint Cookie Murder
Scout Camp Murder
(short story in the Killer Beach Reads collection)
Marshmallow S'More Murder
Movie Night Murder
Mud Run Murder
Fishing Badge Murder
(short story in the Pushing Up Daisies collection)
Motto for Murder
Map Skills Murder
Mean Girl Murder
Marriage Vow Murder
Mystery Night Murder

Greatest Hits Mysteries:
'Scuse Me While I Kill This Guy
Guns Will Keep Us Together
Stand By Your Hitman
I Shot You Babe
Paradise By The Rifle Sights
Snuff the Magic Dragon
My Heroes Have Always Been Hitmen
Have Yourself a Deadly Little Christmas (a holiday short story)

Aloha Lagoon Mysteries:
Ukulele Murder
Ukulele Deadly

Other Works:
Sex, Lies, & Family Vacations

MYSTERY NIGHT MURDER

A Merry Wrath Mystery

USA TODAY BESTSELLING AUTHOR

Leslie Langtry

MYSTERY NIGHT MURDER

Cover design by Janet Holmes

Published by Gemma Halliday Publishing

FROM THE AUTHOR...

This book, MYSTERY NIGHT MURDER is a little nod to two of my favorite mystery thingies: Agatha Christie's amazing AND THEN THERE WERE NONE, and CLUE—the board game (not CLUE—the movie. Never CLUE—the movie).

Agatha Christie is the must-read, go-to author for cozies, and I doubt I'll even come close to her greatness here, but I'll give it a go.

CLUE is the board game I played so often that my siblings ran in terror whenever they saw the box. And yes, I always won. And no, I never cheated. At least…I don't think I did, but then, my memory isn't what it used to be.

I hope you enjoy my little tribute.

—Leslie

Dedicated to the memory of Lori Sweet—the amazing woman who co-founded our Girl Scout Troop and who was a wonderful co-leader for many years.

CAST OF CHARACTERS

The Troop:

- **Merry Wrath**—Ex-CIA agent, Girl Scout leader, and full-time dead body magnet.
- **Dr. Soo Jin Body**—County Medical Examiner—annoyingly gorgeous.
- **Betty**—A feisty 4th grader with issues (far too many to list here).
- **Lauren**—Creative kid with a quirky outlook and penchant for booby traps.
- **Inez**—Clever and resourceful, Inez is the idea kid.
- **Ava**—A natural leader of girls, not afraid to give marching orders (read—*a bit bossy*).

The Girl Scout Council:

- **Stacey Gillespie**—Girl Scout Director of Camps—a real trooper with a positive attitude.
- **Juliette Dowd**—Possible Satan's spawn.

The Guests:

- **Thad and Wren Gable**—Wealthy young couple. Thad is an attorney, and Wren manages an art gallery. Thad is arrogant, and Wren is jittery—which means their marriage is a challenge to themselves and everyone else.

- **Caroline Regent**—A no-nonsense, gruff, middle-aged doctor. Practical to the point of forgetting that there are other people in the world.

- **Dennis Blunt**—Twenty-something trust-fund baby with no goals in life beyond downloading the latest version of whatever video game can keep him from having to work. Coerced into going by parents, who were unable to come.

- **Arthur and Violet Kasinski**—A wealthy couple in their 70s. Generous donors, from old money (well, for Iowa) who love kids but were unable to have any.

- **Taylor Burke**—Forty-year-old first female CEO of one of the largest insurance companies in the world. Was once a Girl Scout and lets everyone know it by saying irritating things like, "That's not how we did it when I was in Scouts."

- **Enos McQuaid**—Nouveau riche. Enos made fast money creating an app that reminds people to brush their teeth. Sold his company for millions. Bored, which is how he got talked into coming.

The Staff:

- **Miriam Cooper**—Housekeeper/cook, in her thirties. Very quiet. Makes a mean lasagna.

- **Ned Odom—**Groundskeeper/handyman, in his sixties. Scary to everyone but Betty.

CHAPTER ONE

"Murder me!" the girl cried out with large, pleading eyes. "Please?"

"No!" begged another. "I want to be murdered!"

I was holding a large carving knife in my hands as I looked these two over. "I'm not going to kill either one of you."

Betty pouted, folding her arms over her chest. "But Mrs. Wrath! You need victims!"

Mrs. Wrath. Sigh. For the past few years, I'd been begging my girls to call me Ms., since I wasn't married. But technically speaking, they were right this time. Sort of. Newly married, my name was actually Mrs. Ferguson. Or at least, it would be if I'd taken Rex's last name.

Lauren objected. "I'm the tallest. I should be the one killed. It only makes sense."

Mrs. Linda Willard, my fourth-grade teacher who had started helping out with my troop here and there, arched an eyebrow in my direction but said nothing. She was learning that my Girl Scouts were, well, a bit quirky.

The girls, who were fourth graders themselves, saw *my* fourth-grade teacher as a sort of mythical creature from the *olden* days, and they viewed her with an awe they'd have for the arrival of Abraham Lincoln dressed in full samurai armor astride a pterodactyl.

Kelly, my best friend and co-leader, gently took the knife from my hands and set it up on a high shelf so the girls couldn't reach it. She should know better. I'd seen these kids form a human pyramid just to get the cookies off the top of my fridge.

"We talked about this," she said sternly (she always said things sternly). "This is a fundraiser for the Girl Scout Council, and we are here to help run it. The adults who paid for tickets get to be the characters and they get to be the victims."

Betty and Lauren simultaneously threw their arms up in the air and stomped away in disgust. I wondered if they'd been practicing that move and finally found a reason to deploy it. Kind of like an angsty, synchronized fury swim.

"We *could* kill *one* of them," I mused. "No point in having the whole troop against us."

Kelly rolled her eyes.

Linda Willard stepped in. "I came up with the mystery for an *adult* victim. I don't think it's a good idea to kill off one of the girls."

Kelly pointed to her and nodded. Mrs. Willard had been her teacher too.

Our former educator was a puzzle master who actually had a New York publishing contract to create crossword books. And when the Council asked me to come up with a murder mystery–night fundraiser, I'd turned to her. She'd helped me solve a mystery recently and was rewarded by the local police with a Medal for Murder. Okay, they didn't call it that. They called it a Citizen's Award for Service. But Medal for Murder would've been way better.

My name is Merry Wrath, and I used to be a spy with the CIA, until I was "accidentally" outed by the vice president of the United States. As Fionnaghuala Merrygold Wrath Czrygy, I had to flee my field assignment to get home in one piece when the news came out. That wasn't easy since I was in a dive bar in Chechnya with a group of paramilitary terrorists who had a thing for CNN (which didn't mean much since that was the only channel they could get besides the current strongman's cable access show on house cats). I barely made it out intact.

Because I was forced into early retirement, the government awarded me a huge settlement before sending me packing. I changed my name to Merry Wrath and came back to my hometown of Who's There, Iowa, to figure out what to do next. Kelly talked me into helping her with a troop, and that was how I ended up in this particular predicament.

Due to a number of *unusual* events, word leaked out about who I really was, and the Girl Scout Council asked me to create a fun mystery fundraiser for their biggest donors. Linda came up with the mystery, clues, and whodunnit stuff. Kelly and I filled in the blanks.

We were going for a sort of twist on Agatha Christie's *And Then There Were None*. One of the board members owned a private island in the middle of a huge lake with a mansion there that we could use. There was no Wi-Fi—ergo, no cheating by looking stuff up on the internet. The players would arrive by boat, and we'd be stranded for forty-eight hours. It was the perfect setup.

The party would start soon. We'd arrived early this morning to help with setting things up. Only eight of my girls were able to come, due to a Monster Golf Cart Rally being held in Bladdersly.

So it was the four Kaitlyns (I have four Kaitlyn M.'s who all look alike for no apparent reason), Betty, Lauren, Inez, and Ava. Dr. Soo Jin Body—the county medical examiner—and I were providing adult supervision because Kelly had to work at the hospital this weekend and Mrs. Willard was going out of town to visit her daughter in Texas. At least they came to help us set up.

And I'd just found out that the four Kaitlyns couldn't stay because they were going to a Weimaraner dog show in Ames. Their mothers, all improbably named Ashley, had started an Etsy shop, making harnesses strictly for that one dog breed. The girls were going along to help and, I assumed, to roll around in puppies.

"Are you sure you can handle it with just four girls?" Kelly bit her lip.

"This is the third time you've asked," I reminded her. "Yes. I've got this. And four girls will be much easier to wrangle."

"I still don't know why they won't tell us who the victim or murderer is," Betty grumped loudly, from across the room.

I ignored it. Kelly and I'd decided that the girls would experience this firsthand. They could try to solve it on their own but had to keep that to themselves. The guests were the stars of this show. Six mega donors who'd paid $10,000 each to be here, these folks were smart and wealthy. They were about to have their socks blown off. Almost literally in fact, since I confiscated Betty's homemade shape charges an hour ago. She'd insisted they were for special effects, but I threw them into the lake anyway.

Other than the four adults (including two employees who lived here), four girls, and eight players, the Council sent two staffers to help. One was Stacey Gillespie, the camp director who my girls loved, and the other was Satan. I'd love to say I'm kidding, but Juliette Dowd was my arch nemesis (and this is from an ex-CIA agent who literally had arch nemeses in the past).

An angry young woman who had a thing for my husband, Juliette tried (and sometimes succeeded) in making my life miserable. I'd wanted to "kill" her off, but Linda said it would be too obvious. She had a point. Plus, Kelly thought I might *really* kill her instead of *fake* killing her, so she decided to remove the temptation for me and edited her right out of the script.

"This house is awesome," I said for the one hundredth time today.

Soo Jin nodded, her beautiful eyes wide with glee. "It's a Queen Anne Victorian! And it's original to the island."

"How do you know that?" I asked. I didn't know that.

She held up a book titled *Islands in the Middle of Lakes in Iowa*. "I found this at the library. I can tell you everything about this place!"

"Is it an interesting history?" I asked. Maybe there was a ghost story! The girls would love that!

Soo Jin flipped the book open and showed me a photo from the mid-1800s. "That's Jim Bentley." She pointed to a scowling man in the photo, standing next to a pretty young woman. "And that's his wife, June. Jim was cheated out of his life savings by a con man from Chicago."

"So he got revenge?" Kelly asked.

Soo Jin shook her head, "No. He developed tuberculosis and was sent to an asylum in Colorado. His wife, June, believed that his poor health was a result of the swindle. I guess they didn't really know what caused tuberculosis back then. Anyway, she tracked the crook down and lured him to the island, to this very house, and murdered him."

"She killed him?" I gaped. "That's an opportunity missed. We could've built a ghost into the script."

The medical examiner shrugged. "It was a pretty straightforward case. June admitted guilt and went to prison. Somebody bought the island after that, and since then it's been privately owned."

"Too bad it wasn't an unsolved mystery," I said. "We could've plugged that in somewhere."

Soo Jin smiled. "That's the only good story in the book. The rest are pretty boring."

I could imagine. A book on islands in lakes in Iowa? Still, I had to give Soo Jin props for preparedness. That combined with her dazzling beauty was a source of aggravation for me. Since it was unreasonable to feel this way, I kept it to myself.

"Okay, everyone!" Stacey appeared in the hallway. The tall woman with blonde hair and a permanent, infectious smile was easily likeable. She ran the Council's camps and was the perfect camp director, always ready with a game or song for the girls to keep them distracted (a talent that made me very, very happy).

She clapped her hands together. "The boat is on its way here with the guests! Those who are staying need to get into their costumes and assume their roles! Those who are leaving should get ready to go!"

Kelly, Linda, and the Kaitlyns waved goodbye and disappeared through the front door. They'd hide in the boathouse until the guests were unloaded and then take the boat back to the shore, where it would remain until lunchtime Sunday, when it would return for us.

The unfortunately named Dead Otter Lake (an improvement on the original Native American name that translated to *Stinky Water Where Animals Die and Men Get Dysentery*) was one of the largest in the state. Just twenty minutes south of Des Moines, in our home county. A very exclusive area, the lake was ringed with giant homes, each one bigger than the next.

Penny Island sat dead center—a small five-acre wooded area with the large mansion in the middle. Our hosts, the

Deivers, handed over their staff and the keys and fled for the *big* city. The only warning was that they had a mini Holland lop rabbit named Gertrude, that lived in the walls.

"She's hiding from us at the moment," Audrey Deivers apologized. "You probably won't even see her while we're gone. We don't even know how she gets in and out of the walls." She went on to say that they'd put a small bale of Timothy hay and a water bottle in the mud room so the bunny would have access to food.

"A mini lop?" I asked. "She must be small."

Audrey gave me a look I couldn't translate. "You'd think so, wouldn't you? But no, it's actually larger than the Holland lop. Which was a huge surprise when she grew."

Upon hearing about Gertrude, the girls launched the greatest manhunt since Jimmy Hoffa, searching high and low (including one rather optimistic search on top of the fridge) but never found the bunny. Audrey told us we might hear her thumping…a thing she did when angry.

"They're here!" Lauren shouted from the front window.

I shooed her and the other three girls up to our room to change their clothes. Soo Jin was waiting for us, already dressed in a fitted skirt, high heels, and an angora sweater with a circle pin. She looked ridiculously stunning. I tried not to hate her for it.

The guests were supposed to arrive dressed in clothes from the 1950s. Linda had wanted to set the party in the '20s, but we couldn't find enough costumes for all of us, so the '50s it was.

The four girls were dressed in sleeveless buttoned-up blouses, pedal pusher pants (that just looked like capris to me), socks, and saddle shoes, with their hair in ponytails tied with scarves. I had to admit, they looked adorable.

As for me, I'd been dreading this moment. Kelly must've thought it hilarious when she brought the giant felt poodle skirt, short-sleeved blouse with Peter Pan collar, and loafers with pennies tucked into them.

"I look like an idiot," I said as I surveyed myself in the mirror. "I'm too old for a poodle skirt."

Soo Jin and the girls looked me up and down. Then my troop began laughing hysterically. I toyed with stuffing them into the walls with Gertrude.

"Okay." Soo Jin approached and looked at my reflection in the standing mirror. "I think I can help."

A few minutes later, Stacey and Juliette burst into the room, each looking very chic in pencil skirts, twinset cashmere sweaters, and high heels.

"You look like an idiot!" Juliette sneered.

Stacey shook her head. "What did I tell you about being negative?"

The redhead simmered but kept her mouth shut. The camp director outranked her. But I knew if we were ever alone, the insults would flow like lava.

The only thing Soo Jin was able to do was apply makeup and do my hair. My normally unruly, short dirty blonde hair had been curled into sleek waves away from my face and with the bloodred lipstick, mascara, and rouge, made me look completely different.

"I think you look amazing!" Stacey said. "You should wear your hair like that all the time."

I scowled at my reflection. Seemed like a lot of work.

"Okay, everyone! The guests are getting settled in the parlor with cocktails. Does everyone remember their parts?"

The girls nodded solemnly. Dr. Body giggled. I grudgingly shrugged, and Juliette disemboweled woodland creatures with her gaze. Okay, that didn't really happen. But in an alternate dimension, several chipmunks exploded.

Stacey and Juliette left the room, and I looked back at the mirror. Actually, it wasn't bad. Except for the ginormous twenty-pound circle of heavy fabric around my waist, I looked okay. Stacey was right about the hair. How Soo Jin smoothed and styled it in a few minutes was beyond me. I probably shouldn't have kept my eyes closed the whole time.

The Girl Scout Council staff was part of the show, as Soo Jin, me, and the girls were. The idea was that the guests were invited to a mysterious party in a house where it turned out the host wasn't present.

There was a housekeeper who cooked and a groundskeeper too. These were played by the actual housekeeper, Miriam Cooper, and actual groundskeeper, Ned Odom. We hadn't had much time to get to know these two, but they were a bit standoffish while we were getting ready. If I had to guess, I'd say they weren't very happy about participating. I wondered how the Deivers had convinced them.

Miriam was maybe in her mid-thirties and seemed normal, just quiet. So quiet that she spoke in a smaller font. Ned, on the other hand, was maybe sixty years old and scary. At six feet, eight inches, he towered (and glowered) over all of us. If I hadn't already memorized the mystery, I'd say he did it.

Stacey and Juliette were playing the parts of two socialite sisters who were also invited. They weren't the victims or the killer but a kind of buffer between us and the guests. Soo Jin and I were playing to type as the leaders of a stranded group of Girl Scouts taking shelter from a raging storm during a failed canoe trip gone wrong. Why the two of us were wearing skirts on a canoe trip had never been explained to us.

And that was it. The guests, whom we were just about to meet, were the real players. We found our way to the lounge—a very large room with four couches, a fireplace, and many chairs. In the middle of the room was a small round table with a large silver tray on top.

"The figurines!" I rolled my eyes. "We forgot them!"

Linda Willard had modelled the event on the Agatha Christie novel, and in the book, as each victim was killed off, a figurine was found smashed. We'd been talking about it for weeks, but I'd totally spaced. Would the guests notice?

Betty and Inez ran from the room and were back before we could yell at them. Betty set a box on the table, and Inez pulled out a very interesting sort of clay rabbit.

"We made these!" the girl said proudly.

One by one, the girls pulled eight Picasso-like attempts at woodland creatures (although I could swear one looked like a hippo) out of the box and set them up in a ring around the tray.

"These are wonderful!" Stacey cried out as she bent close to inspect them. "You girls took the initiative and made these! Good job!"

"All four of us did!" Ava said quickly.

I reached for a disturbingly mutated pigeon, but Betty slapped my arm away. "Leave the squirrel alone," she said.

Squirrel? "They're not exactly dry. How are we going to smash them if they're not smashable?" I asked.

Lauren thought about this for a moment. "We could tear their heads off," she suggested.

Voices came from the front entrance, and we took our places, with Betty shoving the box behind one of the couches. The girls were seated cross-legged on the floor, with Soo Jin and me in chairs behind them.

Stacey stayed with us, while Juliette was greeting the guests. That seemed like having a spider greet flies before eating them. But maybe she was just pure unadulterated evil to me and me alone.

The first to walk into the room was Dennis Blunt. Last week, I'd done my homework and looked up all the donors. Dennis was a sullen rich kid who'd never had to work a day in his life. He'd barely scraped through college, majoring in a degree of his own invention (or rather, based on his parents' generous donation to the school) in video gaming.

If I had to guess, I'd say he was in his early thirties, but it was clear he was embracing a slovenly, slacker image, wearing a black T-shirt with some metal band on it, ripped jeans, and high-top sneakers. His hair was too long to be short and too short to be long, as if he'd found the one hairdresser who could do I-don't-care hair. He looked homeless, not wealthy. But his parents hadn't been able to come at the last minute, so he was their stand-in. Which explained why he wasn't in costume.

Dennis rolled his eyes and sighed heavily as he slunk over to an overstuffed chair and fell into it with a loud groan. He didn't even look at the rest of us, acting as if we weren't even there.

"Idiot," Betty mumbled under her breath.

Thad and Wren Gable were the next through the doorway. A young professional, Thad was well known as one of the leading defense lawyers in the state. Nefariously known. Thad loved making waves, defending some of the worst criminals in Iowa, including the notorious Vy Todd—a convicted smuggler whose path I'd crossed not too long ago.

Thad had a reputation for cheating on his wife, at times openly. His current paramour was going to be here as well. I wasn't sure how that was going to go down. Maybe there'd be a real murder after all.

"Oh." He made a face as he saw the girls. "There are *children* here." The emphasis invoked images of a roach infestation in a sewage lagoon.

Soo Jin put her hand on my arm, probably anticipating I'd say or do something. I relaxed. These folks had given a lot of money to be here. The least I could do was not kill them before they were killed in the game. I made a mental note to have a little *chat* about respect with him later. A long chat that included death threats.

Wren Gable looked at the girls anxiously. "Oh! Well! I guess this *is* a Girl Scout event, Thad," she jittered as she fiddled with some period bangles on her wrist.

Dressed as a well-to-do couple from the '50s, Thad wore a three-piece suit, while Wren was dressed in a dull gray with matching pumps and purse. She tugged nervously on her gloves. Wren was the very definition of a mousy wife. According to my research, no one believed that she was completely clueless about Thad's wandering eye. And yet she never left the man…never even threatened such a thing. Maybe I should have a chat with her too. A long chat with instructions on waterboarding your husband.

Without wasting any more time, Thad breezed past to the liquor tray and poured himself a glass of what looked to be whiskey. Wren fluttered near him as if waiting for permission to sit.

"These may not be the best role models for the girls," I whispered to Soo Jin.

"We can use this as a teaching moment then," she said brightly.

Right. *Girls, don't be like Wren, and don't marry a Thad. And never, ever date a Dennis*. That summed things up.

A grim-looking middle-aged woman entered the room, wearing an unfortunately fitted black dress, ballet flats, and a frown. With short hair and a serious gaze, Dr. Caroline Regent looked like she'd much rather be elbow deep in a patient's intestines. The woman had a brilliant reputation as a surgeon but turned out to be a social dud. My research indicated that, from time to time, she attended galas, but they weren't really her thing, and she rarely talked to anyone.

Dr. Regent had recently pioneered an experimental bowel bypass using snakeskin, making a name for herself nationwide. Unlike Thad, who liked the publicity, Caroline ignored it and spent almost all her time in surgery. I couldn't help but wonder why she was even here.

"Oh! Arthur! Look at the little girls!" An elderly woman with a warm grin came through the door with an equally elderly man.

"This is great!" Arthur smiled at my troop. "I love being around children!"

Arthur and Violet Kasinski were in their late 70s and came from old money. Arthur's grandfather was the first pork producer in the area, a long time ago, and Arthur had built a vast fortune in the hog industry.

The couple were famous for their love of children and were thought to be the nicest people in Iowa. Legendarily generous, the couple had never been able to have kids of their own, so they gave hundreds of thousands of dollars to charities like the Girl Scouts and Boys & Girls of Iowa, among other groups. The two of them were known to be very much in love, still doting on each other like they had when they'd first married. They were the couple everyone wanted to grow up to be.

Arthur and Violet came right over and introduced themselves, asking each girl her name and being delighted by the answer. Arthur rewarded each girl with a cellophane-wrapped butterscotch disk. The girls politely thanked him but didn't seem very sure about what it was. I'd be willing to bet they'd never seen hard candy before. I gave them a quick nod. Betty unwrapped the candy and popped it into her mouth. The smile on her face told the other girls the candy was okay.

Soo Jin and I introduced ourselves last.

"You are so lucky." Violet beamed. "To get to work with kids! I wish I were younger—I'd be a Scout leader every year."

I wanted to say that they might rethink that if they had my troop, but Soo Jin beat me to the punch with a sweet thank-you.

Arthur then reached into his pocket and handed each girl a candy bar. This was familiar territory, and the girls tore into them, thanking them through mouthfuls of chocolate, which amused the older couple and horrified the Gables.

Dennis still hadn't acknowledged the fact that there were others in the room.

The last two people through the door, weren't a couple at all. Taylor Burke was forty, just making Iowa's 40 Under 40 last year before aging out of the award. Petite and imposing, Taylor was the first female CEO of a major insurance company, headquartered in Des Moines. Known to be sharp and very ambitious, she was often called the Dragon Lady of Double Indemnity (whatever that meant). I liked what I'd read about her, especially the part where she'd been a Bronze, Silver, and Gold Award winner when she was a Girl Scout. The only reservation I had was that Taylor was rumored to be Thad's latest fling.

"This is nice," she said as she took in the room, wearing a very red, very expensive vintage designer coat dress. After spotting the girls, she grinned. "And we have real Girl Scouts!" The woman bent down to Betty. "You know what? I was once a Girl Scout too! The youngest Gold Award winner in the state of Iowa."

She said it in a way that complimented herself while insulting us. It was all in her inflection. Most people don't realize how dangerous that can be. In my experience, you had to be careful who you passive-aggressively complimented. You might get away with it with most people, but occasionally you came across a paranoid Lithuanian strongman who thought "have a nice day" was an invitation to a firefight. That's when you're glad you chose to attend his garden party armed with a very, very large handgun. I escaped only because his pet wolf distracted everyone by coughing up a human femur.

Betty must have been suspicious of Taylor's words, because she gave me a cautious look. I nodded, indicating it was okay to respond.

"Okay," the girl said, unimpressed.

Ava, my somewhat bossier Scout, piped up, "That's what I want to be! I want to be the youngest Gold Award winner in the US."

For a split second, a look of annoyance marred Taylor's carefully made-up features, but it disappeared, and she patted the child on the head. "Good luck!"

Clearly, the woman did not like the idea of her record being broken. I decided right then and there that Ava was going to make that happen, if it took all my resources and a couple of well-placed bribes.

"Thad!" Taylor purred when she saw him and made her way to join the Gables at the drinks table.

The man who'd walked in with her had stopped in the doorway and looked around. Enos McQuaid was a bored billionaire and my vote for wild card at the event. Dressed in a work shirt like you'd see at a gas station fifty years ago, the guy seemed to be thumbing his nose at the stylish folks around him.

McQuaid became rich during college when he invented Clean Yo Mouth—a cell phone app that reminded people to brush their teeth. He sold it for millions and then joined the leisure set.

Word on the street said that since he'd retired young, he was incredibly bored and always looking for anything to do. He'd been parasailing with Canadian geese…in Nicaragua, skateboarded illegally down the Pyramids of Giza, and built a castle for zombies in his backyard (violating zoning laws and scaring his neighbors into wondering what he knew that they didn't). What the twenty-seven-year-old was doing here was anyone's guess. The man scanned the room, his gaze lingering on each and every guest, before he found a chair and sat down.

"Now that everyone's here," Stacey announced, "it's time for introductions! I'm Stacey, and you've already met Juliette." She indicated the redheaded demon, who simply nodded to the guests but managed a sideways sneer at me. "Why don't we go around the room?"

"If I have to." Dennis sighed. "Dennis Blunt. My parents made me come. Otherwise, I wouldn't be here."

Wren didn't give us time to react to this. "Wren Gable!" She pulled on her husband's arm. "Wife of Thad Gable. I'm excited to be here!" She turned to kiss her husband on the cheek, but he shot her a look that would've seared her lips off, so she stopped.

"Thad Gable." He sneered. "I'm sure everyone knows who I am."

Lauren raised her hand. "I don't know who you are."

"Well, you're just a kid," he said. "Ask your parents. They know who I am."

Betty piped up, "Are you a serial killer?"

Thad jumped, spilling his drink. "Why would you think that?"

"Because that's the only reason we'd know who you are," Betty suggested.

To be fair, it made sense to me.

"No," he said as he refreshed his drink. "I'm not. But I defended one."

Inez frowned. "You had to defend a serial killer? From police or bad guys?"

"No…I…um…" Thad struggled to find an answer.

"From ninjas?" Ava's eyes grew wide.

"I didn't defend him from ninjas!" Thad shrieked. "I defended him in court!" He sat down and scowled at the girls.

Arthur stood up, smiling at Violet, who remained seated. "I'm Arthur Kasinski, and this is my lovely wife, Violet. We have a large farm not far from here, and we are so happy to be here supporting the Girl Scouts. Right, honey?"

Violet nodded her agreement as Arthur sat down. She looked serene and happy. They both did. Was that how Rex and I would be fifty years from now? I hoped so.

"Enos McQuaid," the young man said as he struggled to stand. While not grossly so, he was definitely overweight. "I was an inventor. Now I'm a man of leisure." He looked around awkwardly.

"What's a man of leisure?" Inez asked.

"Maybe it's a planet?" Lauren asked. "Are you from another planet?"

Enos shifted his considerable weight from one foot to another. "No, it means I have lots of free time. I don't really work. Not anymore."

"What did you invent?" Ava asked.

He looked relieved to have a subject he understood more than he understood little girls. "It's an app on your cell phone that tells you when to brush your teeth."

The girls looked at each other then turned toward him.

"Is it for stupid people?" Betty asked. "Because everyone knows when to brush their teeth."

Lauren spoke up. "Maybe it's for babies. Babies don't know when to brush their teeth."

Ava rolled her eyes. "Babies don't have teeth!"

"Or cell phones," Inez added.

"Well..." Enos looked confused. "I guess there are enough people who needed reminding, or I wouldn't have been able to sell it for millions."

The girls immediately started whispering among themselves. My guess was they were trying to invent something no one needed so they could make millions too.

Taylor got to her feet. "I'm Taylor Burke, and as you all know, I was one of Iowa's 40 Under 40 Top Business Leaders last year, was just named CEO of the Year by *Insurance Magazine* and was the state's youngest Gold Award winner." She shot Ava a quick glare. "And when I was a Girl Scout, we didn't do silly things like this. We camped in tents we made out of whatever we could find, and we lived off the land. Girls now have it too easy."

I was pretty sure Taylor never did any of those things when she was a Scout. In fact, she probably lied to earn badges quickly and made others do chores for her. Maybe I'd invite her camping with my troop sometime. My girls made the twins in *The Parent Trap* look like amateurs.

Did these people know each other? The introductions implied that they didn't. In fact, the only recognition between guests had been Taylor and Thad. These people had to know each other, at least marginally, since the number of major donors in Des Moines was probably limited.

"Hi, everyone!" Soo Jin's voice next to me gave me a start. "I'm Dr. Soo Jin Body, the medical examiner based in Who's There, Iowa."

I waited for the usual drooling to start. Soo Jin was willowy with perfect skin and glossy black hair in a sleek bob. Her sweet nature was genuine, leading men and women to fall for her. I kept my eyes on Thad, who didn't disappoint as his eyes went up and down her figure. Wren didn't notice, but Taylor did. And she did not look happy.

Enos's eyebrows went up hopefully. "You're playing the part of the coroner?" He probably hoped he'd be a victim.

The lovely doctor blushed. "Oh! No! I can see where that might be confusing. I really am a medical examiner—but not a coroner. I'm not here in any professional capacity. I'm just here to help with the troop." She indicated the four girls on the floor in front of us.

"What's the difference?" Enos asked.

Soo Jin smiled. "It's an easy mistake. The titles seem interchangeable, but they aren't. A coroner is an elected official and doesn't have to have any medical degree. Whereas a medical examiner is a real doctor and is a hired position."

The guests looked at each other in surprise but said nothing, then, as a group, turned their attention to me.

I struggled to get to my feet under the weight of the felt circle skirt. "I'm Merry Wrath, the leader of this troop. We're just here to help."

Wren's jaw dropped. "You're Merry Wrath? *The* Merry Wrath?"

"Well"—I was famous?—"I'm *a* Merry Wrath."

She turned to her husband. "Thad! This is the woman I was telling you about! Mike Czrygy's daughter!"

Ah. They knew my dad, Senator Czrygy. Everyone knew him. He came back to Iowa and visited as many of the 99 counties as he could whenever there was a recess. An important politician who chaired many committees, Mike Czrygy was considered one of the most powerful members in the Senate.

Thad looked at me with interest for the very first time. "The spy who was outed and came back to Iowa?"

I nodded, unsure what to say. Even though word had gotten out about me, I'd been incognito for years. Unfortunately, bodies popped up around me like ants at an all-sugar picnic, and when my senator father was in town for my wedding a couple of months ago, people started putting two and two together.

One of the reasons I loved Iowa was that people weren't really starstruck. Celebrities, good or bad, weren't a big deal. They were just like everyone else. No one had confronted me about my past since word leaked out. And I liked it that way.

"I heard about you." Enos stared at me. "Your name was Finn something."

"Czrygy," Wren corrected.

I held my hands up. "I'm just Merry now. And I'm just here with my troop to help out. That's all."

Most of the guests seemed okay with my plea. But something in the eyes of Caroline Regent caught me off guard. Had I met the doctor before? I think I'd remember any reconstructive bowel surgery. But the look passed, and I chalked it up to my overactive imagination.

"My friend," Dennis said unconvincingly, "is writing a book about you."

I froze. A book? About me?

He nodded as if I'd said those words aloud—which was super creepy. "Yeah. About how you were a spy and stuff."

Someone was writing a book on me? Why on earth would they do that? First off, almost all of my cases as a field agent for the CIA were and still are classified. Secondly, I wasn't really that interesting. Someone once wrote a Hollywood script about me, and it did not go well.

"Who?" I demanded. "Who is writing a book on me?"

Dennis shrugged.

"I need a name, address, phone number, and social security number. Now." If he thought I was dropping this, he was wrong.

"It's none of your business," Dennis said.

"None of my business? Your friend is writing an unauthorized biography on me! I'd say that's my business." I started to get up, but Soo Jin put her hand on my arm.

She whispered, "Not here, not now. This is a fundraiser, remember?"

As much as I hated to admit it, she was right. This wasn't the time or place. You might be interested to know that the right time and place was a dark alley with a baseball bat and no witnesses.

Dennis wiggled his eyebrows at me, and I sent him a look I hoped would make him swell up and break out in boils.

It didn't.

Stacey clapped her hands together. "Not here at the moment are Miriam, the housekeeper, and Ned, the groundskeeper. They work for the Deivers family and will only be involved in meals and that sort of thing. They aren't part of the game." She took a big breath. "Now that we've all introduced ourselves, before lunch is served, let's go over the ground rules."

I heard her tell the group that they were playing characters based on themselves but set in the 1950s—just so we wouldn't have to remember new names and character backgrounds. But it was fuzzy because in the back of my mind, I was wondering when I could kidnap Dennis, tie him to a chair, and torture him for more information on this buddy and her book.

There was a shed outside. Which probably meant there was rope, hedge pruners, and a convenient amount of flammable bug killer that I could use to get answers. Don't get me wrong. I'm not a paranoid person. It's just a spy thing.

We don't like our exploits published for all the world to see. Especially the stuff we get wrong. Like the time in Nicaragua when I accidentally kidnapped Pablo Escobar's (no, not *that* Pablo Escobar—it's a common mistake since this Pablo was his cousin three times removed) pet sloth. How was I to know that Honeybun had crawled into my jeep for a nap?

By the way, Honeybun is safe and living in a sloth preserve in Costa Rica. Like I was going to take her back to Escobar! Sure, it put a price on my head for 10,000 Cordoba Oros (which, sadly, is only about $300 in the US), but it was worth it because Pablo wasn't known to be kind to anyone due to an unfortunate hemorrhoid issue, and I got to play with the baby sloths while I was there. I'd have to take my troop sometime.

But as much as I wanted to deal with this now, Soo Jin was right. I had to focus on what we were doing. I'd feel awful if the other guests said screw it, wanted their money back, and went home. I wasn't going to give up on this, but I wasn't going to deal with it now. Eventually, I shook myself out of my funk and started to listen as the staff, Miriam and Ned, appeared in the doorway.

"Ned here," Stacey was saying, "will show you to your rooms upstairs, where your luggage has already been delivered. Once you've unpacked, join us back down here for further instructions."

Everyone got up at once and made their way into the hallway. There was a grand staircase in the center of the house that led up to our rooms, each one with their own bathroom. The two couples had two rooms, and the Girl Scout employees shared a room, but the four single individuals had their own rooms. Soo Jin and I had a room with two twin beds and two sets of bunkbeds. Ned and Miriam had a separate cottage out back.

The Deivers didn't have children, which made me wonder about the room with bunk beds. But I couldn't think of a way to ask without sounding nosy (an annoying spy trait, says Kelly), so I didn't. Maybe they had family who came to visit. Or maybe they rented it out on Airbnb. Or perhaps the room was for Gertrude, the lop-eared bunny. It didn't matter, because it suited us perfectly.

Once the guests were gone, I waited for the girls to pepper me with questions. They'd guessed a while back that I'd been something like a spy, but for reasons I don't completely understand, we'd never really talked about it.

"I don't think it's a good idea that someone is writing a book about you," Inez said somberly. "What if they find out how many people you killed and make you stop being our leader?"

Ava scowled. "That's not going to happen. Not on my watch."

"Hold on," I said in my defense. "I haven't killed all that many people."

Soo Jin shot me a warning look.

"I mean," I added, "I haven't killed *any* people." It was a lie, but I should probably avoid telling them that when I was in the CIA, I killed exactly five people. Not all at once. I'm not that good.

"Want me to torture it out of him?" Betty asked, a bit too eagerly.

"You have to put a bar of soap in your sock and hit him with it," Lauren nodded. "You don't leave marks that way."

I shook my head. "No one is doing anything of the sort. These people donated a great deal of money to support the Girl Scouts. Trust me, I'll find out what's going on with this book my own way." Which would most likely include pliers and some painfully applied Q-tips.

Lauren turned to Inez. "I'll bet she uses a car battery and cables. That's what *I'd* use."

Betty shook her head. "Waterboarding. Best way to find out if your brother has been stealing your Halloween candy, hands down."

Soo Jin was familiar with my girls and used to this kind of talk, so she ignored this part of the conversation. I faded back inside my own head, trying to wrap my thoughts around this book thing. Maybe Dennis was messing with me. He was a bored brat who didn't want to be here anyway. Maybe he was doing it to get back at his folks. In any event, I was going to get him alone and find out.

That was when we realized that Miriam was still standing in the doorway. The woman was so quiet and unobtrusive she might as well be invisible. Her expression was unreadable, so I had no idea what she thought of what she'd just heard.

"They're joking." I laughed artificially. "They love to joke."

Miriam just blinked.

The girls stopped talking like Spanish Inquisitors and chattered amongst themselves about what they thought would be for lunch. The unanimous hope was for chili cheese dogs and ice cream. To be honest, I was rooting for that menu myself.

Soo Jin and I talked quietly about the script. She knew the premise and story but not who the victim and killer were. Stacey and I were the only ones who knew that. We were careful not to spill any secrets aloud. The girls didn't know what was going on, and we thought it best if they didn't. Then it would be fun for them. Plus, they couldn't randomly announce spoilers to the other guests—something Betty had become very fond of in the last six months. I haven't seen a movie since because I now knew things I wish I didn't. Perhaps we should stage an intervention the next time a Marvel's Avengers movie comes out.

After a few minutes, the guests began trickling into the parlor, quietly taking up their former seats. I watched everyone, sizing them up for the part they'd play. That was when it occurred to me that this was a very odd group of numerous ages and interests.

When they got to their rooms, each person should have found a sealed folder with their personal information in it—who they were, if they were victims or the killer. I couldn't tell if any of them had read it or not. Had there even been enough time?

Once everyone was seated, Miriam seemed to come alive. Well, she blinked. She took one step into the room and said, "Lunch."

The game had begun.

CHAPTER TWO

No one spoke…we all just sat there, frozen to the spot, wondering if Miriam had actually said anything or if we'd imagined it. Her voice was so soft it was practically nonexistent.

"Did she say something?" Betty asked.

Ned scowled and in a deep, gruff voice, shouted, "LUNCH!"

We all stood up immediately. For a moment, I thought the girls might be intimidated, but then I remembered who I was talking about and put that concern aside.

The dining room was just across the hallway. The house was a huge white Victorian with a wraparound porch, complete with swinging wicker benches. The inside was another matter. Laid out like a square, there were nine rooms around the perimeter, with the staircase in the middle.

Once inside the front door, on your left was the lounge in the corner, with the kitchen at the other end and the dining room in between the two. On the other side of the kitchen was the ballroom, and on the other side of that was the conservatory, also in the corner. The billiard room was next, and then there was the library, and the other corner had a study, which was to the right of the front door. There was a grand hall between that and the lounge that had the main entrance in it.

The layout seemed strangely familiar to me, but I couldn't place it. It reminded me of my elementary school—long since closed down. That building was also a square with the gym in the middle. That must be why it was familiar.

We filed out of the lounge and walked into the dining room. There were seats for twelve, and Miriam had set up a kids' table in the corner. The girls sat without complaint, which made me wonder if they knew something I didn't. They were picky eaters who preferred to eat nothing but PB&J sandwiches and ice cream novelties. Even at camp. Which made a refrigerator a necessity at most campsites.

It occurred to me that I hadn't seen the menu for the weekend. Had I given Stacey suggestions? I couldn't remember. If I had, we'd probably be eating a lot of junk this weekend—something these high-end donors wouldn't appreciate.

Still, Audrey Deivers had spoken highly of Miriam's cooking, so whatever it was should be pretty good. No one said a word as Miriam and Ned brought out plates, which they set before us. We seemed to be having some sort of fish, hopefully not caught in Dead Otter Lake. The filet was blackened and accompanied by a small salad.

This was disappointing. I wasn't a big seafood (or in this case, lakefood) fan. The salad only added insult to injury. Looking around the table, I realized that the guests weren't terribly impressed. That wasn't a good sign. We had a great mystery planned for them, but you couldn't investigate on an empty stomach, even if it was only pretend.

Once we were all served and our water glasses were filled, Miriam brought out a covered tray and set it in the middle of the kiddie table. The girls were grinning ear to ear, as if they knew what to expect. She lifted the lid, and I started drooling.

"Grilled cheese!" Ava cried out as she grabbed a gooey sandwich and started munching.

I raised my hand to ask if I could have a grilled cheese sandwich, but Miriam had disappeared into the kitchen. Would the girls notice if I snagged one? My stomach rumbled at the thought of toasted bread and melted cheese.

"Can I have your attention?" Stacey hit her water glass with a spoon.

As the guests turned to her, I reached out to the kids' table to snatch a sandwich, only to be met by an empty plate. I withdrew my hand and picked up a fork to play with my salad.

"I'm so glad you're all here," the blonde continued. "Each one of you has been very generous in joining us for this adventure. Girl Scouts is an amazing organization where girls find empowerment and fun!"

"Where are the sandwiches?" I whispered to the girls. They shrugged as they chewed.

"Hopefully"—Stacey smiled—"you've each received your envelope with your information for the party. Please don't share what you have with anyone else. That way we can all have fun finding our killer!"

There was some vague enthusiasm from the men, but the women leaned in eagerly. I picked at my salad, hoping it would fill me up a little. If desperate, I would attempt the fish…but that was only as a last resort.

"When do we start?" Taylor asked. She cast a look at the girls. "When *I* was a Girl Scout, we had to make our own lunches over an open fire. Doesn't that sound like fun?" Somehow she'd made this sound like an insult.

Four little girls looked at her curiously. We were on dangerous territory because my kids were expert fire starters. Maybe I should check the house for matches. Hiding them would be tricky since my girls were bloodhounds when they wanted something sniffed out. I have never been able to keep cake in my house.

Juliette attempted a smile that looked more like a trembling snarl. "Right now. We began the minute we sat down to lunch. And we will conclude in two days, at lunch on Sunday."

"I read my file," Wren tittered. "This is going to be so much fun!"

Violet agreed. "This is a wonderful story line. And thank you for keeping our characters close to real life. We don't have to memorize any names!"

Dennis sighed heavily. "When does the victim die?"

"Stick to your script," Dr. Caroline snapped. "And don't give anything away. I don't like spoilers!"

Dennis rolled his eyes. I had a feeling that would be his number one reaction from here on out.

"What do we do now?" Arthur asked.

Stacey shrugged. "You have lunch. Chat with the other guests. The killer and victim know what happens next. We just wait and see."

There was an overbearing silence, pierced by the clatter of forks on china. I guess eating was preferable to making small talk. And why weren't there any rolls? There should be rolls. I could eat that if I had to. I started to rise from my chair, when Ned came into the dining room and set down a basket covered by cloth.

Snatching up the basket, I reached in to find hard breadsticks. They were thin and barely counted as food, but I still took five. Now if I could only score some butter…

Betty marched up to Enos. "So, *Clean Yo Mouth* is your app?"

McQuaid nodded, unsure how to communicate with a child.

"I still don't get it, but my dentist says it's the best invention since the cavity."

"Oh. Thanks." He gave her a halfhearted grin and turned back to his food, hoping she'd go away.

She didn't. "I have some thoughts that would improve it," Betty pushed.

The young man turned to her, his eyes bulging and mouth hanging open. "Well, I've sold it. It belongs to someone else now…"

Betty was undeterred. "I get that an alarm goes off when it's time to brush your teeth, once in the morning and once at night. And then there's a little song that plays so you know how much time to brush."

"Okay?" Enos wasn't sure how to respond.

In fact, he was looking a little green around the gills. What kind of idiot goes to an event for Girl Scouts if he's terrified of little girls?

The girl pretended to press a button on her cell. "I think you should deliver an electric shock to the person, instead of alarms. And keep shocking them, upping the voltage, until they brush their teeth."

Every head turned towards Betty now. I had to admit, the idea had merit. On sleepovers, lock-ins, and camping trips, it was nearly impossible to get the girls to brush their teeth. Mental note: buy a stun gun.

"I'm not sure that's possible?" Enos squeaked.

Betty was not confounded. "It is. If you use Taser technology. I tried it on my brother's phone. It worked pretty well until Mom confiscated it."

Soo Jin began to choke, causing Dr. Regent to run over and pound her on the back. I was surprised she didn't go for the intestines.

"That's, um, interesting?" Apparently Enos could only answer in questions. The poor guy was starting to sweat profusely.

Lauren joined them. "You could make a cell phone case with a hidden switchblade that activates if it doesn't detect the smell of mint."

Betty rolled her eyes. "That's just *stabbing* them. Shocking them will make a bigger impact."

She had a point.

"This is ridiculous!" Thad growled from the other end of the table.

Enos and Thad were at each end. From there it was boy-girl around the table. "Let's get a move on. Would the victim just die already?"

Betty and Lauren shrugged and went back to their table. I watched as Betty yanked her napkin off her plate, exposing a hidden grilled cheese sandwich. My stomach rumbled as I watched her devour it.

Wren's hand fluttered to her throat. "Thad," she said quickly. "There's a plan in place. I see no reason why we shouldn't—"

Taylor cut her off. "I agree. I'm here to play the game, but time is money, so I'll ask a little question. How are all of you on your life insurance?" She concluded with a wink aimed at Thad.

"What's life insurance?" Inez asked loudly.

Lauren turned to her. "When you die, your family gets a lot of money."

"And then there's double indemnity." Ava nodded. "If they're murdered, you get twice the payout."

Taylor's eyebrows went up. "That's true. Smart girl."

Betty cocked her head to one side. "Then why not murder the guy? Then you get more money."

Ava shook her head. "Not if you're the killer. If you are the killer and the beneficiary, you get nothing."

All adults were staring at the children's table, which was located in the corner near Thad. I got it. I usually found the girls' interactions amusing too. In a way, I was proud of them for their curiosity about things. Well, except for fires. And weapons. Oh, and grilled cheese sandwiches that they didn't share with their leader…

Taylor regarded Ava—the girl who wanted to break her record on being the youngest Gold Award winner in the state. I couldn't tell if she was impressed or angry. Or both.

"How do you know so much about insurance?" she asked.

Ava shrugged. "My mommy sells insurance. For your company. Sometimes I read the brochures."

"You and I"—she pointed at the kid—"should talk."

Ava was about to comment, when she frowned, focusing on something at the other end of the room. "I think the game has started."

"Why do you say that?" I asked. I knew for a fact that it wouldn't start until after lunch.

She pointed. "Because that app guy is dead."

We turned to look and saw the girl was right. Enos McQuaid was face down in his fish. My heart began to pound as Wren and Violet clapped with glee and Dennis showed interest in something for perhaps the first time in his life. Arthur and Caroline nodded as if they saw this coming all along.

There was only one problem.

Enos McQuaid wasn't supposed to be the victim.

CHAPTER THREE

The guests immediately started talking, excited that the game had begun.

"What is it?" Soo Jin asked me.

I whispered, "*He's* not the victim."

She leapt to her feet and raced over to the man. She felt his neck for a pulse and then, looking at me and with an imperceptible movement, shook her head.

Stacey froze, a mask of fear on her face. She and I were the only ones who knew the story. Enos wasn't the victim. Dennis Blunt was. And right now, Blunt emerged from his haze of indifference to pull some papers from his pocket. He read them and looked at Enos before reading them again, just in case he'd missed something.

I joined Soo Jin and spoke quietly. "He's really dead? Did he have a heart attack?"

She nodded. "He is dead. But I don't know about the heart attack. Could you clear the room for me?"

"Okay, everyone," I announced. "Let's all move to the ballroom."

"Oh good!" Violet squealed. "Time to interview each other and take notes!" From her purse she pulled a small notepad that we'd provided in the envelopes and clicked the end of a pen. The others noticed and did the same thing.

I gave my troop a look. "That means you too, ladies."

The guests practically ran through the doorway. My troop grudgingly followed them out. Last week, they'd offered some creative suggestions on gory deaths for the *victims*, including sausages, gummy brains, and blood made from cake icing and food coloring. I reminded them that this was a cozy mystery and that kind of thing wasn't allowed, which disappointed them immensely. When they came up with a way one of the victims could "explode," showering the room in pieces of flesh-colored fondant, I had to end the conversation by bribing them with ice cream. By the way—that always works. Always.

"Stacey," I said, "you and Juliette go with them. Keep an eye on things until we get there."

The woman stood stock still. Juliette approached. "He's really dead, isn't he?" The look on her face indicated she thought, or hoped, that I'd done it.

"Yes. And he wasn't the victim. But don't tell anyone that. Just go to the ballroom and keep an eye on things until we get there."

The two women agreed and left. Soo Jin took out her cell phone and tapped in a number. She frowned and tried again.

"I don't have any cell service here."

I hit Rex's number on speed dial. Technically, we were outside of Who's There's jurisdiction, so I should've called the sheriff. It was force of habit that made me call my husband when someone dropped dead in my presence.

The room was growing darker. Glancing out the window, I noticed that several dark clouds were covering the sun.

"I've got nothing." I stared at my phone. "Oh, right. Audrey told us the cell service here was practically nonexistent. Wait! I think there's a landline by the stairs."

She nodded, and I ran out of the room.

BOOM! There was a clap of thunder. A storm? We weren't supposed to get bad weather. A very elaborate gilded vintage phone was on a credenza next to the staircase. I picked it up.

Dead. No ringtone. Had the storm knocked out a telephone pole somewhere? I wasn't really sure how that worked.

Back in the dining room, I reported this to Dr. Body. She was taking pictures of the deceased, using her cell.

"We can't call out?" She frowned. "We'll have to send Ned and the boat for help."

Rain and wind began to lash at the windows. I turned to exit the room, but the doorway was filled with the large and angry-for-no-reason Ned Odom.

"What's going on?" he barked as he loomed over me.

"Enos McQuaid is dead." I pointed at the body. "We have no cell service, and the landline is out." A crack of lightning lit up a room that was becoming darker with the storm. "We need you to take the boat to shore and call the sheriff."

He shook his head. "I can't."

"Why not?"

"Boat's gone," he roared. "Your people took it to shore but didn't bring it back. Just got something on the radio in the boathouse. Storm's too bad."

A radio! "Contact the authorities using the radio!"

The big man shook his head angrily. "It was just hit by lightning. Radio's out."

"Are you serious?"

"Of course I am!" And without another word, he left.

I stood there, mind racing. Enos must've had a heart attack. And there wasn't anything we could do. Something nagged me from the back of my mind, but I ignored it. The only way to make a call was back at shore, where cell service worked. We needed to get there, but how? And what were we supposed to do in the meantime?

"Merry." Soo Jin waved me over. "Help me get him to the floor."

We each took hold of one of the young man's shoulders and lifted him off the chair, which pulled his face out of the fish. With my foot, I slid the chair back, and we laid him out on the floor. And that was when I saw it.

My heart sank. "This was murder, wasn't it?"

Soo Jin nodded. "Looks that way."

McQuaid's skin was pink. Like he was covered in Pepto-Bismol pink. There was a slight odor of bitter almonds. I assumed Enos had been poisoned, because people didn't usually look like that unless they were covered in bubble gum. How did I know that? Because I had a troop of little girls who made an unfortunate choice one night at camp.

"I'm fairly certain he was poisoned," Soo Jin said, pointing at his skin. "See the unnaturally pink skin? Cyanide can do that. Check his food."

I studied his plate. It had the same things as everyone else's—the fish and the salad. Both half-eaten. The other plates were similar. Apparently, the lunch wasn't that popular with our guests. That wouldn't look good on the exit evaluations.

Soo Jin was opening the man's mouth. With a fork, she gently pried his lips apart and reached inside. She pulled out a piece of the fish and set it down.

"We all ate the same lunch." I gasped.

She gave me a look. "You didn't eat your fish."

"Yes, but you and everyone else did. And no one else is dead."

I moved to a point between the two doorways, facing the lounge and the hallway to keep watch in case one of the other guests returned. There was a flash of movement in my peripheral vison on my right. Someone was in the lounge.

Great. Now people were just wandering around. I marched into the room to find it dark and empty. I could swear I'd seen a shadow. But unlike the dining room, there was only one entrance to the lounge. So, I would've seen anyone coming out.

The five large windows were all locked from the inside. Rain lashed violently at them, followed by a few softer claps of thunder. After checking behind curtains and the furniture, I gave up. Enos's murder caused me to imagine things. I passed the table with the clay figures on it and froze.

"Soo Jin!" I shouted as quietly as possible. "Can you come in here?"

"I shouldn't leave the body," came the reply before she appeared in the doorway.

The look on my face must've convinced her, because she quickly walked across the hall.

"What?"

"Look!" I pointed at the tray full of mangled clay animals. The head of the squirrel-like thing had been torn off and was lying in the middle of the tray. The body—or at least what I thought was the body—lay on its side.

And that was when it hit me what had been bothering me.

"This is just like the book!" I whispered.

She frowned. "The book?"

"Agatha Christie's *And Then There Were None*." I took a deep breath. "The guests are stranded on that island due to a storm. As people die, the figurines are destroyed."

Soo Jin nodded. "Yes. I know. That's why Mrs. Willard wrote the script this way. When the victims die, the girls are supposed to come here and break the animals."

"Yes, but the girls didn't do this. They were with us. And we weren't expecting a storm. We were told there was no cell service here, but we weren't expecting the landline being unusable. And we certainly didn't expect someone to really die. And it wasn't supposed to be Enos."

The medical examiner looked around her. "There has to be something different."

I nodded. "There is one thing. In the book the power goes out. At least we don't have that to deal with."

Another crack of lightning and blast of thunder and the lights flickered. After a split second, all the power went out.

Soo Jin raised her eyebrow. "You were saying?"

We went back into the dining room and found that not much had changed with Enos. I was kind of hoping he'd spring to his feet and shout "Ta-da!" He didn't.

"What do we do with him?" I asked as Ned and Miriam showed up with candles, which they placed around the room. I waited for them to leave. "We can't leave him here," I whispered loudly after they went into the hall.

"I'm not sure." Dr. Body bit her lip. "We shouldn't put him in his room. With the power out, things are going to warm up, especially on the second floor. He needs to be on ice. And the fridge in the kitchen is too small."

"Maybe they have a chest freezer in the basement?" I suggested.

She snapped her fingers. "The basement. It's probably cooler down there. We'll do that."

I hoped Ned would return, and I toyed with asking Thad and Dennis for help. But Soo Jin didn't want to contaminate the body. So, we lugged Enos into the hallway, keeping an eye on the ballroom, and dragged him to the door in the side of the staircase that led down to the cellar.

The man was heavy. Maybe two hundred and fifty pounds that didn't look great on a five-foot, five-inch frame. I weighed about 120, and I was pretty sure Soo Jin weighed less than that. It wasn't easy moving him, and for a moment I entertained the idea that we could sort of set him on the top step and roll him down.

But like Soo Jin said, we couldn't contaminate the body, which probably included adding bumps and bruises that might confuse her inspection later. Instead, I took his arms and she took his legs, and we went down step by step. I couldn't guarantee that we didn't hit his head a few times along the way, but I'd warn her about unexpected bruises later. Besides, the pink skin and odor of bitter almonds made it pretty obvious he'd been poisoned. Soo Jin agreed but asked me to be careful nonetheless.

I hadn't been in the basement, and I was pretty sure no one in our group had. It wasn't in the script. Fortunately, the Deivers had never finished it. And it was dry. We dragged him to a corner of the cement floor and laid him out.

"Mrs. Wrath!" screamed a girl upstairs, and the two of us raced up to see Betty just outside the door.

She pointed at the lounge, and I took her meaning.

"The squirrel," I said quickly. "We know."

The other girls were peeking out of one of the ballroom's four doorways. Behind them, I could see the other guests talking, as if they didn't just witness a murder.

"We have to tell everyone," Soo Jin said. "I can't see any way around it."

I agreed. "I guess that means it's over."

The medical examiner shook her head sadly. "I guess so."

"Okay." I squared my shoulders. "But we aren't going to say Enos was murdered. One of those people killed him, and we can't let that person know that we're onto him."

Soo Jin agreed, and I walked toward the doorway as the girls backed away. Inside the large ballroom, clusters of guests were interviewing each other animatedly. Except for Dennis. He was in a corner, staring at the papers he'd consulted earlier. The snarky smugness he'd displayed earlier had been replaced by real confusion.

Stacey and Juliette were in the other corner, next to the piano. Stacey was horrified. Juliette looked grim (but then, she always looked like that). No doubt they were worried about liability. Too bad Enos hadn't died from a heart attack. It would make things so much easier.

"What are you going to say?" Soo Jin whispered.

I didn't answer. Instead, I clapped to get their attention. Thirteen pairs of eyes turned my way.

"I'm so sorry," I said. "But Enos McQuaid is dead."

A clap of thunder rumbled outside, and the rain was coming down in crashing torrents that almost drowned me out.

"Yes, dear," Violet said. "It's part of the event. We know."

Caroline Regent cleared her throat. "It was pretty convincing too. I thought he was really dead."

"Did you know our cell phones don't work here?" Wren looked anxiously around her.

Arthur smiled warmly. "The special effects so far are amazing. You ladies have done a smashing job."

A round of applause broke out, aimed at me. Dennis looked around, startled, and then joined in. He probably thought we'd changed things up.

"Um…" He held up his hand. "I think I got Enos's envelope by mistake."

The room grew quiet. I could see how he thought that. Maybe he went to the wrong room and picked up the envelope for Enos by mistake, in spite of the fact that I'd written *DENNIS* on it in large letters.

"No," I fumbled. "You didn't."

By now the other six guests were confused.

"Dennis was supposed to be the victim," I said. "Enos is *really* dead. That wasn't part of the event."

"That poor man!" Wren howled.

"Well, he was super fat," Taylor mused.

The others gasped.

"What?" she asked. "He was."

Caroline nodded. "I've seen that a lot in my work. Fat builds up around the intestines. Leads to strokes and heart attacks."

Arthur put his arm around his wife. "It was a heart attack?"

I thought about how to answer this, but Juliette cut me off. "Yes. It was from natural causes."

There was a brief silence as the guests weighed their options. Why did Juliette say that? Oh. Right. Stacey didn't know it was murder either. Maybe that was a good idea—letting everyone think it was natural causes.

"We should go," Violet finally said. "I don't care if you keep the donation. I just don't think it's right to continue."

Thad groused, "I'm going to ask for *my* money back."

Wren looked like she was about to disagree but thought better of it.

"You can keep my parents' money too," Dennis said.

Taylor scowled. "Well, they're not keeping mine! Especially after *that* lunch!"

The group started moving toward the door, mumbling about collecting their things and leaving.

"I'm sorry," I shouted. "But we can't leave just yet. As Wren mentioned, there's no cell service. The landline is dead, and the boat is at the shore. Ned says the water is too rough from the storm."

Betty pipped up. "We could do semaphore. I could climb onto the roof and wave some towels."

I immediately regretted the badge work we'd just done on semaphore. While the offer was consistent with the Girl Scout values of helping out, the thought of Betty falling off the rain-soaked roof was almost too much to bear.

"It's too dangerous," Soo Jin said. "But that was a great idea."

As long as nobody panicked and the power came back on, we'd be fine for the couple of hours or so until the storm blew over. I just needed to keep everyone safe, and we just needed to keep it together and hunker down. We were all adults (well, mostly), so this shouldn't be too difficult, right?

Wren began to wail. Loudly. She went off like a distressed siren. Caroline patted her awkwardly on the back, but her husband, Thad, did nothing to comfort his wife. Instead, I was pretty sure he copped a feel from Taylor's backside. I couldn't really see it, but I was familiar with the move, due to some unwanted advances from a Japanese businessman at a barbecue in Tokyo.

"You have to get us out of here," Taylor menaced, ignoring Thad's touch. "I don't want to stay another moment in a house with a dead body."

The others seemed to agree.

"Well," I said. "You're all welcome to go outside and stand in the cold rain with the dangerous lightning." I was talking to them like they were children. Actually, my girls were the only ones remaining calm, and they seemed to want to stay.

My offer put a stop to any mutterings. At this point, all of the guests (except for the killer) believed that Enos died of natural causes. They weren't worried about a mystery killer.

The problem was what to do in the meantime, because I had no idea how long this storm would last. What would Rex do? My husband, the detective, would investigate. This was the perfect situation since the killer might not even realize that Soo Jin and I were onto them.

There was a rattling of dishes in the dining room.

"Please," I called out. "Just stay here for now."

Soo Jin was hot on my heels as I ran into the dining room. Ned and Miriam were inside, gathering up the dishes. Did she know about the murder? Ned only knew we had a *body*, not a *victim*. He must've told Miriam what happened to the young man.

"Wait!" I ran over and took Enos's plate from her. "We have to check the food!"

"It wasn't the fish," the woman said defensively. "I made it myself. It wasn't the fish."

"I know." I was pretty sure someone poisoned the fish—which would mean it *was* the fish. I just didn't want to tell her that. "I just wanted to see something."

She nodded and then took an armload of dishes across the other hall, into the kitchen.

Soo Jin examined the plate. I had no idea what to look for. At last she shook her head. "I don't see anything different." She ran into the kitchen and returned with a large baggie. The medical examiner then put the plate and all of its contents inside and zipped it shut. She waited for Miriam and Ned to leave before asking, "Where should we store evidence?"

That was an excellent question. None of the other guests knew about the basement. But Miriam and Ned did. Where else could I put it where it would be safe until the authorities arrived?

"Is Miriam a suspect?" she whispered. "She made lunch. We know she handled the food and set the plates before everyone."

I stared at the doorway. "I suppose she is. She had opportunity. I remember her giving Enos his food. But what's the motive?"

As far as I knew, Miriam and Enos wouldn't know each other. There was an age difference, and they definitely ran in different social circles. Unless Miriam really didn't like brushing her teeth, I couldn't think of anything that would make her want to kill him.

"Do you think there's some sort of connection between Miriam and Ned?" I wondered out loud. "Father and daughter maybe?" Ned was in his sixties. I was fairly certain about that. "Or May/December romance?"

Soo Jin shrugged. "There may be no other connection besides working together."

Miriam returned, so we stopped talking.

"I'm sorry I was defensive. I didn't want to serve fish. I was going to make lasagna." She was wringing her hands and glancing over her shoulder toward the kitchen. "I make an excellent lasagna. The Deivers would have it every day if they could."

Lasagna would've been amazing. My stomach rumbled in time with the thunder outside. With the power off, we wouldn't be able to cook anything.

"Maybe we can have it when the power's back on," I suggested.

"We have a range," the cook said. "One of those cookers they have in England. It runs on thermal heat and is always on. Can I make you a plate?"

Soo Jin and I shouted at the same time, "Yes!"

"Heat up the whole thing," I insisted. "Everyone will love it."

The housekeeper went back to the kitchen, a little happier. We could feed the guests some real food, and that might distract them. And I could watch everyone to see if one of our guests might be the killer.

Soo Jin headed to the ballroom to make the announcement that lunch was back on, while I did a quick search of the place where Enos had sat. We were probably taking a risk in being poisoned if Miriam or Ned was the killer. But I was starving, and besides the girls, who'd eaten an entire platter of grilled cheese sandwiches, I was sure everyone else was too.

The chair looked like the others, and I examined every part of it, including the underside. I wasn't sure why…it just seemed like something a detective would do. Lifting the place mat revealed nothing either. Nothing. I couldn't find any evidence of the poisoning.

While everyone glumly filed in to take their places at the table, I slipped across the hall to the kitchen to keep an eye on Miriam while she heated up the lasagna. The scent of pasta, marinara sauce, sausage, and cheese drove me mad with desire. I found the box of breadsticks on the counter and helped myself.

The kitchen was pretty large. Larger than the one in my little ranch-style house. This room had all the bells and whistles, from granite countertops to stainless appliances to the odd stove Miriam was working at.

"That's a range?" I asked through a mouthful of crumbs. "It's kind of weird."

In her insanely quiet voice, the cook told me that this was an AGA range—something the English kept at their country homes. Constantly warm and not connected to power, the range could cook multiple things at once in its four compartments and on the hot plates.

As she spoke, I poked around the cupboards, looking for a big bottle with a skull on it, labelled *POISON*. I didn't find it. Ned wasn't around either, but by the way Miriam kept glancing at the doorway, I guessed he was coming back any minute.

The rain pounded the windows, and even though it was daylight, I could barely see five feet outside the window. How did we miss the weather reports when we set this up? I hoped that task hadn't been assigned to me.

Miriam prattled on almost soundlessly as I thought about what had happened here. We had eight guests, two staff, two Girl Scout Council employees, and my troop. Immediately, I eliminated my group from the list of suspects. And even though it would be awesome if Juliette were the murderer, I was pretty sure that she and Stacey were innocent. Juliette might hate me with a burning passion, but she loved her job. It was her life.

One of the guests was dead. That left nine suspects. One of those people must've poisoned Enos. But who was it?

CRAAAAAACK!

A bolt of lightning blazed through the room, and the ground shook. Peering out the window, I could see that a huge branch had been sheared off of an old maple and landed a foot away from the window.

And in the room across the hall, a killer was quietly sitting with my troop, convinced they'd gotten away with murder. We were trapped on an island with no cell service or power and no way back to the mainland.

One of those people murdered Enos McQuaid in cold blood.

But who was it? And why?

CHAPTER FOUR

The lasagna was a hit. Miriam might be skittish and talk like a whispering child, but she did make an amazing lasagna. I was at a point that if I didn't eat soon, I'd be no good to anyone.

Stacey and Juliette brought the drinks cart in from the lounge. It was a little early to start drinking, but then again, alcohol often went a long way to loosen up tongues and lower inhibitions. And since I'd be detecting on my own, lower inhibitions seemed like a plus.

Soo Jin and I stuck with water, and the girls had juice boxes that I checked for tampering—just to be safe. Almost everyone else had a cocktail or two. Even Stacey and Juliette had a glass of wine. Good. Stacey was looking a little pale. Every time the thunder clapped, she jumped. I couldn't blame her. She was genuinely worried about Enos's untimely demise and probably that these people were in danger. The fact that this was a Council fundraiser would come secondary to Stacey, and I loved her for that.

People ate like there was no tomorrow, which hopefully, for everyone here, there would be. Was Enos a one-off or just the start of a killing spree? I shuddered to think about that. I had my troop to worry about. My thoughts went back to the moment Enos entered the room. Had someone been waiting for him? Did the guests know in advance who would be here? That might be a good place to start. Murderers usually take out people they know.

I couldn't remember anyone looking at the app designer with recognition. Was Enos targeted specifically or just in the wrong place at the wrong time? And how was I going to find out?

We needed to find the killer fast.

"So," Soo Jin whispered in my ear. "I'm convinced it's cyanide poisoning."

A chill ran through me. Cyanide had a brutish reputation in the spy world that went back to the Cold War. As an agent, my one fear was of being poisoned. It was a legitimate concern, since poison is the weapon of choice for despots, maniacs, and this underwear model I'd worked with in Ulaanbaatar.

I was also afraid of being robbed by monkeys. I was only ever in India once, but that little beast was armed with a piece of broken glass and took my purse. Somewhere in the jungle, there's a monkey carrying a black leather bag filled with aspirin, tissues, some money, and a mint tin jerry-rigged with a sound-sensitive explosive that was set to blow when it heard me whistle "Mah Na Mah Na" from *Sesame Street*. Fortunately, there were no monkeys or underwear models here, which was a relief.

"So someone here is packing one of the deadliest poisons imaginable. Great," I said quietly.

The girls were in their corner, eating lasagna—which made me wonder, since they'd already eaten their weight in grilled cheese. The kids were not talking—their eyes were watching us at the adult table.

My Scouts weren't lightweights. They were brave and clever and could handle just about anything. I say "just about" because I did recently find the chink in their armor. Centipedes. Not one of my girls would go into a room with a centipede in it. Apparently, Betty told the others that if you get bitten by one, you swell up with helium and float away until you burst. I really should talk to her about that.

"How long do you think this storm will last?" I murmured.

Soo Jin shrugged. "Not a clue. We don't have access to the internet or phones, and meteorology is a bit out of my skill set."

The buzz of low murmurs came from the table. No one seemed really panicked. Since they didn't know Enos was murdered and thought he died of somewhat natural causes, there wasn't anything to fear. And with the body in the basement, it was out of sight, out of mind.

My gaze landed on each guest. Who was the killer? The sullen slacker, Dennis? The egotistical, ambitious Taylor? The gruff and socially awkward but brilliant bowel surgeon, Caroline Regent? Obnoxious Thad and timid Wren? Or the sweet elderly hog farmers, Arthur and Violet?

Then again, it could be Miriam or Ned. But they were permanent staff to the Deivers family. They weren't new to this or participating in the game. Still, I couldn't rule them out until I knew for sure.

From the flirtatious looks they gave, it was pretty obvious that Thad and Taylor knew each other. Everyone else appeared to be strangers. But was that actually true? Did one of them know Enos and want him dead? Believe me—I'd rather have that than a psychopath who killed randomly.

What was the right approach here? Ask point blank if any of them were acquainted? That would seem suspicious since they all thought Enos had a heart attack. I had to be subtle. Use my espionage skills. Ask questions designed to flatter that would give me the most information. I was a bit rusty.

I looked at Soo Jin. She was part of law enforcement, and as a medical examiner, she had to know police procedure. It was a good thing I was stuck here with her. Maybe she'd know what to do next.

"Are you uncomfortable?" Soo Jin asked. "You keep tugging on your skirt and frowning."

"Yes. I would like to get out of this ridiculous costume." The poodle skirt was heavy and itchy. And I did not like wearing dress shoes.

Soo Jin tapped on her water glass with a spoon. "Hey, everyone!"

All heads turned toward the stunningly beautiful doctor.

"Since it might be a while until we can leave, when you're done eating, why don't you get out of these costumes?"

Heads nodded as everyone agreed. Everyone but Dennis.

He frowned and said, "What do you mean?"

"Costumes. We're wearing costumes." Taylor sneered. "Well, *we* are."

Chairs scraped against the polished hardwood floor as the guests started to leave the dining room and head for the stairs. I took the opportunity to eat another piece of lasagna before making my way to our room. Granted, I knew that Miriam was working on dinner, but what if the killer targeted her?

"We're fine in these clothes, but we should all go up to the room together," Betty announced.

"Good idea," I said.

Once inside, Soo Jin carefully hung up everything she took off as soon as she removed it. My skirt was on the floor in seconds. The moment I was in a pair of jeans, tennis shoes, and a black T-shirt, I felt better able to cope with what was happening. Ava rolled her eyes and began hanging up my clothes. I'd have to thank her for that later.

"That app guy was murdered, right?" Lauren asked. "Betty told us about the squirrel."

I thought about lying to them but didn't. It was important for them to be safe and on the lookout.

"Yes. Enos McQuaid was murdered."

Betty sighed. "Just when I was going to pitch my idea for a set of earbuds that double as a flamethrower."

The other girls patted her back sympathetically. Flamethrowers in earbuds? Did she have diagrams? I'd kind of like to see that.

I motioned for everyone to join me. "You guys are going to have to stick together, if you can't be with me or Dr. Body. There's a killer in the house. I don't think we're targets, but who knows?"

"Merry!" Soo Jin looked shocked. "Don't frighten them!"

"They have to be on their guard." I turned back to the girls. "But no one knows this besides us. Okay? The murderer might know that Dr. Body and I know Enos was killed. But you need to act like you don't know."

Ava spoke up. "Right. We *know*, but we don't *know*. Got it."

"Yes," I agreed. "That's it exactly."

Inez scratched her chin thoughtfully. "Which means we'll make good detectives."

Lauren nodded eagerly. "No one notices little girls! We can do all kinds of snooping!"

Betty and Ava cheered, but I shut it down.

"No snooping! At least, not without me."

Soo Jin shook her head. "No snooping at *all*."

"She's right." I sighed. "But keep your eyes open. If you see something unusual, you need to tell one of us, okay?"

Inez scratched her chin. "I think we need to pinky swear not to tell anyone what we know."

A cheer went up as all of us got into a circle and pinky swore. This was good. The promise of a pinky swear was unbreakable. I had yet to meet a kid who didn't follow that rule to a T. If only it worked with grown-ups. I could've used that in my job on numerous occasions. *Pinky swear that you won't tell your boss that I took the nuclear plans! Pinky swear that you won't reveal that the sim card is hidden in that package of Oreos! Pinky swear that you won't tell your cousin, the drug lord, that I accidentally killed his favorite chicken!*

Once the ritual was complete, we went back downstairs as a group. I spotted the flicker of candles in the lounge. The rest of the guests were standing around the tray with the seven upright animals and the broken squirrel. Oops. I should've gotten rid of that.

"Is that supposed to be us?" Thad pointed at the lumps of clay.

"It's like the book!" Wren whined. She wrapped her hands around her husband's left arm, but he didn't seem to notice because with his right hand, he was lightly touching Taylor's backside. Didn't anyone else see this?

Why on earth hadn't I taken the tray and tossed it? The broken sculpture kind of gave the murder away.

"I broke it." Betty stepped forward, and the three small heads behind her nodded. "I was playing with it, and I guess I wasn't very careful."

Arthur smiled. "Ah. That settles it." He patted the girl on the head and offered her a butterscotch. "Good for you for admitting it. You don't know your own strength, do you?"

"He has no idea," I murmured to Soo Jin.

"You broke the armadillo?" Caroline asked.

Stacey piped up, "No. It's a squirrel." She gave the girls a knowing wink.

"Looks more like a bat with four legs to me," Dennis grumped.

Betty narrowed her eyes. I knew that look and got between them. "Maybe you should all just sit down."

The guests relaxed and took their original seats to wait out the storm. Betty had bought us some time, by confessing. This was a gift, and we couldn't waste it. But where to start?

Stacey motioned to Juliette, who didn't move, and then walked over to me and Soo Jin. "I think I'll help in the kitchen."

Juliette stayed where she was. Even though we'd all changed into casual clothes, she was wearing a green polyester slacks suit. She was always wearing green. And while it was charming that she loved her job that much, I couldn't help but wonder if she slept in pajamas decorated with Girl Scout logos, or serial killers. The woman noticed me staring and gave me a dangerous look.

Usually Juliette jumped at any opportunity to humiliate me in public. Over the past couple of years, she'd screamed at me in front of my troop and others. Why was she different here? Was she overwhelmed by Enos's death? I was pretty sure she'd have a party if it had been me lying in the basement.

"I'll go with," Soo Jin told Stacey. "Inez, Ava, why don't you girls join us?"

The two girls nodded and followed the women out of the room. They were on the case.

Betty and Lauren asked if they could use the bathroom. Even though I wasn't sure that was their destination, I had no choice but to allow it. What were they up to? I stood in the hall, watching as they made it to the bathroom near the stairs. Once I was certain they were where they said they'd be, I turned back to the room.

Now…where to begin?

Thad and Taylor were having a serious conversation about something that seemed to require them licking their lips a lot. Gross. There was no point talking to them because I knew that they knew each other. Caroline Regent was studying a painting over the mantel, and Wren was chattering to the Kasinskis.

"And there's a poem...'Ten Little Indians,'" Wren said as I approached. "And each line in the poem predicts how someone will be murdered."

Violet nodded. "I remember that rhyme! Ten Little Indians went out to dine. One choked himself, and then there were nine!" She clapped her hands with glee.

Wren's eyes grew wide. "That's it! You have an amazing memory! And when someone dies, the figurine is stolen or smashed or something. I can't really remember that part."

Arthur frowned. "But Enos died of a heart attack. And Dennis was the intended victim. Why break the figurine?"

"Because Betty confessed to breaking it," I cut in quickly.

Violet laughed. "*Someone's* memory isn't as good as mine!"

Her husband laughed. They were a jolly couple. And yes, that's a strange way to describe someone who isn't Santa.

Wren continued, "The poem was in each guest's room. That was the connection." She sat back as if she'd just solved the whole game, even if we weren't playing.

"Did any of you know Enos?" I tried to sound casual.

The elderly couple thought about this for a moment, but Wren piped up.

"I didn't, but I think Thad knew him." She nodded at her husband, who was glaring at her from across the room. Had he heard her?

"I don't think we've ever met him before today," Violet said at last. "I've never seen him at any of the fundraisers we've been to."

"And he certainly isn't a Pork Producer!" Arthur added, referring to an organization for pig farmers. They called their wives Porkettes. And every summer they elected a Pork Princess. I am not kidding.

Enos might not be a Pork Producer, but his bacon was definitely cooked.

I shrugged. "I just wondered. I hadn't seen him before either. I thought it was nice of him to come and donate to the cause though."

"Even though I didn't know him," Wren chirped, "I'd heard of him. He's into experiences. It's a millennial thing."

Arthur looked surprised. "What's a millennial thing?"

Violet looked confused. I guessed that she didn't know either.

"It's this generation of young adults," I said. "They're supposedly more into experiences than stuff. They'd rather go sky diving than buy a nice car."

"Oh that. I guess I've heard that generation called millennial." He scratched his head. "But if they spend all their money on skydiving instead of buying a car"—Arthur still didn't get it—"how do they drive to work?"

All three looked at me expectantly. Somehow I'd become the expert on this.

I shrugged. "I guess they think life is too short to work all the time. They'd rather get out there and do stuff."

The old farmer shook his head. "But that's what you do! You build your future with hard work. When you retire, you can travel and so forth."

Violet patted his hand. "Each generation is different, dear. Our generation had different priorities."

Her husband slapped his knee. "That's right! We had the war! We saved money and spent wisely! And we didn't need an app—whatever that is—to tell us how to brush our teeth!"

The man was getting agitated. I wondered if he wasn't the killer. Farmers used cyanide forty years ago to kill vermin. Grandma Adelaide Wrath once got a visit from the sheriff when it had been discovered she'd had enough cyanide to take out the whole county. Turned out, the poison had been very old and she'd never known how to dispose of it. Fortunately, she'd kept it safely stored in strong metal barrels—that were taken away by the authorities. But for a long time, the sheriff made sure he stayed on her good side.

It was very possible that Arthur had access to the poison in one form or another. I just couldn't think of a way to ask if he had brought a deadly toxic substance with him to this event.

"I know," Violet said calmly. "But the times have changed. Young people can live how they want to in peacetime.

I'm glad there isn't a war to fight. Maybe skydiving is their way of living on the edge."

"Were you in World War II?" I asked Arthur. It seemed rude not to acknowledge his participation in a major world event.

"Oh no!" He smiled, his eyes crinkling in the corners. "I was born just before World War II. Still…" He looked off into the distance. "I would've played my part if I'd had the chance."

His wife beamed at him and squeezed his hand. They really were adorable. Still, I couldn't take them off my list of suspects just yet. Violet turned to ask Wren more about the book, and the two women went on as if this odd break in the conversation had never happened.

"Excuse me," I apologized. "Must mingle!"

Caroline was still staring at a painting on the mantel. Or she'd fallen into a standing coma for no reason. Either way, she was alone, and I approached her because a doctor could certainly have access to cyanide.

The painting was abstract—a riot of purple and yellow squares with red and green triangles on a blue background. A small plaque on the frame read, *Sleepy Kittens.*

"Nice!" I pretended I understood what the hell I was talking about. "Do you like art?"

She didn't look at me but said, "It looks familiar. I can't place the artist. What do you think it's saying?"

I had absolutely no idea, but one thing I've learned about discussing art—anything goes. There are no wrong answers. Once, in Greenland, I convinced a roomful of people that the watercolor painting of apples was a comment on the rise and decline of anarcho-syndicalism. I got a standing ovation. I still think it was just a painting of apples, and I still don't know what anarcho-syndicalism is.

"It's obviously about anger," I said calmly.

The doctor nodded. "I agree. I think I see shades of jealousy too. Possible notes of death."

"You're an art aficionado," I offered. "Do you go to a lot of openings?"

She turned to me as if she finally noticed I was there. "No. But my undergrad degree is in art history."

"Have you been to the Des Moines Museum of Art?" I persisted. "They had an opening last fall on Incan gold."

"I never go anywhere," she said as she turned back to the painting. "I don't much like people."

Then why was she here? Was she the killer? Saw an opportunity to kill Enos and signed up?

"Were you a Girl Scout?" I pressed.

"Yes," she said. "A long time ago. I barely remember it."

I tried another line of inquiry. "Too bad about Enos. I'm sorry it ruined the event."

Caroline turned to me and looked as if she wanted to say something. The wheels were turning behind her eyes as she sized me up. Underestimating her would be a mistake, I realized.

"That idiot should've taken better care of himself. He was prone to health issues."

"Oh?" I tried to dampen my rising enthusiasm. "So, you knew him?"

It was as if I'd just reached over and slapped her on the face. Her mouth dropped open. "No. Why would you think that?"

"You said he was prone to health issues…I thought…" I started, but she cut me off.

"No. I didn't know him." The woman stormed away in a huff.

I'd hit a nerve. But then again, she might always be this way. I didn't have any reference point to start from. The doctor had been gruff since she walked in the door. Did she really dislike Enos, or did she feel that way about everyone? And how was I going to find out?

For a moment I toyed with having my girls commit art fraud by whipping up a bunch of abstract paintings and drilling Caroline on what they meant. But that seemed to be a lot of work, when I could just throw her to the floor and stand on her neck until she started confessing. Torture was something I could handle.

Dennis was slumped in a chair, staring at a cell phone that wasn't working. I decided to take a chance and talk to him. Since she stormed away in a huff, I knew Caroline wasn't going to be approachable again for a while.

I put on my most sympathetic face and sat down beside the man. "I'm so sorry, Dennis, that it didn't work out. I'm sure you were excited to play the victim."

Sure, this was incredibly insensitive since a man had died. But I was pretty sure Dennis would think this was just about him. Which made me realize, this might rule him out as the killer. Why give someone else the attention if you wanted it for yourself? Was I already ruling him out?

"Yeah, well, whatever." He didn't look up.

"I'm hoping we can do it right next time." Faking sympathy for an idiot like Dennis was not my favorite thing to do.

He scowled. "I won't be here. I'm only here because my parents couldn't come. I'm glad we're leaving early."

"I am sorry. Did you know Enos well?" I soothed.

"Kind of," Dennis mumbled.

He knew him? Now we were getting somewhere! I wasn't sure where that was, but it was something more than nothing. Right?

"I'm sorry for your loss," I apologized again. "Was he a friend?"

"No. I was supposed to invest in that toothbrushing app. I guess I dragged my feet too long because he shut me out and went with another investor."

Aaaaand…there it was. Dennis thought his loss was that he missed out of a chance to make money—not that an acquaintance had been killed. I wondered how upset he'd be if Enos had been a friend.

"That's rough." I nodded.

"It was for me." Dennis narrowed his eyes at me. "How long are we going to be here? I could be home playing *Fortnite*."

Was that a motive? Could he have killed Enos to avenge his missed opportunity? Was the confusion over Enos dying when *Dennis* was supposed to "die" just an act? I kind of hoped it was because it would make my day sending this slacker to prison. I was pretty sure they didn't have *Fortnite* there. Still, Dennis was lazy. Planning and executing a murder took effort—something I wasn't sure he was capable of unless it involved a couch and a pizza.

I shook my head. "I have no idea. We don't have TV, internet, a working radio, or cell service. Hopefully it'll be over soon."

He went back to staring at his phone. This conversation was over. For a moment I thought about asking him point blank if he killed Enos—but no one knew he was murdered, except for the killer. The truth was my ace card, and I wasn't ready to throw that away yet.

Which left Thad and Taylor, who were now arguing about something. I couldn't decide if it was better to cut in when they were emotional or wait until things calmed down. And seriously, did they not realize how obvious their affair was? Those two had been side-by-side since Taylor showed up. Either they didn't care or were foolish enough to think they were being discreet.

A quick glance at Wren, who was deep in conversation with Violet, told me the woman was completely oblivious. In fact, most of the guests seemed to be a bullet short of a full magazine.

And where were Betty and Lauren? Just as the thought popped into my brain, the girls walked through the door, wearing huge grins. I knew that grin. Those two were definitely up to something. I motioned for them to follow me into the hall.

"What did you do?" I turned on my Inquisitor's voice.

The Inquisitor voice is the best tool in a leader's box and works for things like, *Who put a frog in my water bottle? Why are there two dozen Canadian geese in the pool* (usually followed up with, *And why is all the bread gone)?* And *Where are all the boxes of matches?*—where the Inquisitor voice sounds more like the Terrified and Panicked Leader voice.

The girls looked at each other and then said at the same time, "Nothing."

I folded my arms over my chest in a weak attempt to look more menacing. "You know, that's kind of creepy."

"We know," they said, perfectly in sync.

"You're making it worse!" I threw my arms into the air. "Where were you, and don't say the bathroom."

Betty leaned forward. "We were doing a little snooping in the guest rooms. Did you know they've all packed their bags but left them in their rooms?"

Lauren added, "Like they expected someone else to carry the bags for them?"

"It makes sense. Their bags were taken up to their rooms. They just expect Ned to take them to the boat. But that's beside the point! You weren't supposed to snoop!" I glanced into the lounge to see if anyone heard us, but no one seemed to.

"Do you want to know what we found?" Lauren wiggled her eyebrows.

This was a quandary. Yes, of course I wanted to know what they found. No, I didn't want to encourage them.

I gave in. "What did you find?"

That was when I noticed that Lauren was holding something behind her back.

"Give it." I held out my hands.

Lauren handed me a piece of paper. It was similar to the poem in Agatha Christie's book—but changed to reflect the fundraiser.

Eight little Girl Scouts on a trip with Kevin,
One ate some bad fish —
And then there were Seven.

Seven little Girl Scouts whittling some sticks,
One was careless with a knife—
And then there were Six.

Six little Girl Scouts went to swim and dive,
One drowned in the lake—
And then there were Five.

Five little Girl Scouts headed for the shore,
One fell down a flight of stairs—
And then there were Four.

Four little Girl Scouts climbing on a tree,
One was crushed by a branch—

And then there were Three.

Three little Girl Scouts messing with some glue,
One sniffed the bottle—
And then there were Two.

Two little Girl Scouts sitting in the sun,
One got roasted—
And then there was One.

One little Girl Scout joined the CIA for fun,
She went undercover—
And then there were None.

The CIA? "Where did you find this?" I demanded. "And what does that thing with Kevin mean?"

Betty shrugged. "There's a copy in each room. On the floor, like someone shoved it under the door. I don't know who Kevin is, but maybe that's a clue?"

Lauren considered this. "Maybe he meant Heaven? Or eleven?"

"On a trip with Heaven?" Betty shook her head. "That doesn't work! Although on a trip with eleven might fit."

"Like eleven Girl Scouts," Lauren answered. "Or seven." She snapped her fingers. "Maybe it's 7-11! The girls are going to a convenience store!"

"I like Kevin better," Betty decided. "And it gives us a name for the killer."

The other girl nodded. "Nice alliteration too. Kevin the Killer."

"Or Killer Kevin," Betty added.

Lauren said, "I think we agree that this is more of a Kevin-based thing."

"Okay," Betty said. "We'll keep it Kevin."

I didn't argue with them because I kept reading the poem over and over, trying to find answers beyond the great Kevin-Heaven-Eleven debate.

The poem was spookily apocryphal. After all, Enos did eat some bad fish, after which, he died. And even worse—the rhyme indicated that all eight guests were targets. Were we dealing with a serial killer who liked poetry and whose name might or might not be Kevin?

The last line was about going undercover for the CIA. According to the poem, and if he succeeded, I was the last victim. It wasn't farfetched for the killer to know about me. Word had started leaking out months ago. And it wouldn't be difficult to find out I was going to be here. Still, it was very creepy to be singled out in the murder poem.

And that was where Kevin the Killer screwed up. Many bad guys had tried to kill me before, and they'd failed. And they were professional spies, assassins, and a chicken armed with an Uzi.

If Kevin thought killing me was going to be easy…he had another think coming.

CHAPTER FIVE

I pulled Soo Jin aside and showed her the note.

"These are in each room?" She scanned the poems quickly.

I called Lauren over and asked.

"Every room," the little girl said.

"The girls found them on the floor, just under each door," I mused. "I'm gonna go out on a limb and say no one else has seen these yet."

Which meant that these were shoved under the doors after people had packed to leave here. Why didn't the killer do it earlier—before lunch maybe? Perhaps he didn't have time to manage it unseen.

"This doesn't make sense." Soo Jin frowned. "Eight refers to the eight guests. But the last one might be about you. Which means one of the guests will survive."

I nodded. "Because one of the eight is Kevin the Killer. He won't kill himself."

Soo Jin's eyebrows went up. "Kevin the Killer?"

"The girls liked the alliteration." I shrugged. "It helps to have a name."

A thought popped into my head, and I asked Lauren, "You didn't go out and investigate the staff cottage, did you?"

She shook her head. "Want us to?"

Ned and Miriam weren't with us. If one of them, or both, was the killer, then whoever investigated their cottage would be in danger. Besides that, the storm had picked up some serious steam. I didn't want the girls to get hit by flying debris or lost in a blind driving rain.

"No. Stay here. Keep an eye out for anything suspicious," I said as Soo Jin, Stacey, and the other girls returned to the room.

As Lauren walked away, I studied the poem. "Look." I handed the poem to Soo Jin. "The next one is a stabbing."

"At least they're warning us." The medical examiner sighed.

I was sure she never thought she'd have to examine real dead bodies during the event.

The poem was a sign. The killer wanted us to squirm…and he was doing a good job of it. If the poem was a warning, we should see a stabbing next, followed by a drowning and a bad fall down the stairs. As long as I kept people away from sharp objects, bathtubs, and the staircase, we might stand a chance.

My head was spinning. Something had to be done right away, but what? I was torn between tipping off the killer by announcing the poem—but that would require telling the others that Enos was murdered.

On the other hand, acting like we didn't know what was going on might make the killer lower his guard. If we collected all copies of the poem and kept them away from the guests, Kevin might get angry enough to do something stupid. I wasn't sure if that was a good thing or a bad thing.

What was the right way to handle this? Announce Enos's murder and freak everyone out, or keep it all hidden, possibly provoking Kevin into action. And should I keep referring to the killer as Kevin—or should we come up with another name, like The Bastard Who Wants to Kill Us All?

"Do you think the last target is you?" Soo Jin asked quietly.

"It looks that way."

But I had no connection to any of these people. Why kill me? Okay, so I wasn't new to the concept. People had tried to kill me before. Fortunately, I'd survived those attempts. But what if my luck had run out? Frankly, it would be embarrassing if someone finally took me out at a Girl Scout meeting instead of in a dark alley in Mumbai or at an international sad clown festival in Paraguay (but that's a story for another time).

The idea that this was some deranged psycho killer killing for fun was not good. Trying to find a killer who didn't have a motive, other than *kill everyone in the house*, made things much harder. How could you find a killer who killed indiscriminately? He had the methods listed in the poem, but did he have a plan for who died how?

For now, I had to go on the suspicion that the targets were premeditated. That someone was getting revenge on eight people. If there was a connection, I could find it, couldn't I? I'd solved murders before. Okay…sometimes the solution just fell into my lap. And I often had help from Linda Willard or Kelly.

None of this made me feel any better. I had a room full of people who thought Enos died of natural causes. Was it fair of me not to warn them? I couldn't guard everyone at once. But they could be cautious when on their own. And if I didn't tell them and more people were murdered, it would kind of be my fault.

I made a decision.

"Folks," I announced loudly, "I have to tell you the truth."

It got very quiet.

"Enos didn't die of natural causes. He was murdered…"

There was an audible, collective gasp.

I looked each and every guest in the eye. "…by one of you."

It should come as no surprise that the room erupted in screaming chaos. As I studied each person, they all seemed to be genuinely terrified. The killer was a good actor. This made it much, much harder. But what did I expect? For Kevin to stand up and confess, maybe throwing in an apology for good measure? Hmmm…that idea had merit.

As the realization hit, it was as if someone let a drop of water hit the middle of a pond. Everyone stepped back to distance themselves from the people around them. The elderly couple stayed together, but the rest pulled apart. No one wanted to stand next to the possible killer.

"How do we know it's not Miriam or Ned?" Taylor called out. "Or one of you!"

Caroline scowled. "Who pays $10,000 to kill people?"

"We're being hunted!" Wren wailed.

Betty appeared with a stack of papers. Without permission, she'd run off and collected every copy of the poem.

"What are you doing?" I hissed. "It's dangerous!"

She shook her head. "No it's not. Everyone is in here. The killer isn't out there."

She had a point, but she was wrong. Ned and Miriam weren't here. I really needed to check those two out.

"I don't care. You girls will stick to me and Soo Jin. Got it?" I took the papers from her.

The poem. The guests should know about it. Keeping information from them would be a bad idea. I clapped to calm everyone down.

"We found one of these in each guest room." I handed them to Ava, who nodded and started handing them out. "I think it's from the killer."

They read in silence, the blood draining from their faces. Not one of them smirked, looked guilty, or gave themselves away in any other manner.

"Kevin?" Dennis asked, but no one responded. Apparently only Dennis and I thought the mention of Kevin was odd.

Thad looked at me. "Does this mean the next murder will be a stabbing? How are you going to protect us?"

That was a very good question.

"I'm going to have to frisk you," I said at last. "And while I'm doing that, the girls will search the room for hidden knives."

Without another word, the kids each took a corner and started working their way around the room. They looked a little too excited for my comfort. Weren't they afraid? Oh wait…they weren't in the poem, other than the *little Girl Scouts* part. And the killer had no idea we were incorporating real Scouts into the show. That decision was made late in the game.

"How do we know you aren't the one who murdered Enos?" Dennis asked. "According to my friend who's writing the book, people drop dead around you all the time!"

"Fair enough," I said, thinking that Dennis and I were going to have to have a chat about his "friend." "Dr. Body can search me before I search you."

"She could be in on it!" Taylor screeched.

"She's a medical examiner! Which means she's practically a cop," I protested. "Believe me—she doesn't want to have any more murders here."

Caroline stepped forward. "I agree. I think we should all agree that Dr. Body is innocent."

"You're just saying that because she's a doctor!" Wren whined.

The surgeon stuck her chin out. "That's right. She's a colleague. But she's also an investigator." She turned to me. "And you can frisk me next."

Soo Jin stepped up and began to pat me down. "I hope you know what you're doing," she mumbled.

"Of course I don't," I replied.

"Then," Dennis said, "I think she should be the one to search us all."

There was a general agreement in the group. It was a good idea. People would certainly trust her more than they'd trust an ex-spy. Soo Jin agreed.

After all of my limbs, torso, and shoes had been felt up, the medical examiner walked over to Caroline and started her search. To my surprise, the other guests formed a line, each waiting for their turn. I watched them to make sure someone didn't try to hide a knife.

The problem with searching everyone was that this house had knives in the kitchen. This killer would have no problem taking one at almost any time. I'd have to clear that room of all pointy weaponry. Hopefully, Miriam wouldn't need knives for whatever she had in store for dinner.

The girls took their job seriously, turning over every pillow and cushion, opening every book, and Betty even felt the inside of the fireplace. It was when she pulled the lid off a marble urn and stuck her hand in, pulling out a handful of ash, that I realized she'd gone too far.

"Betty! Stop!" I called out.

She frowned at her hand. "Why do they put fireplace ashes in this thing?"

I motioned for her to join me, keeping my eyes on the guests. "That's not fireplace ashes. See?" I pointed to a small brass plate on the lid.

"*Grandpa*?" Betty asked.

I nodded. "I think that's someone's cremains."

"Cremains?"

Lauren started giggling. "It's when they burn a dead body until it's ashes! You stuck your hand in someone's grandpa!"

Ava looked shocked, but Inez joined in on the laughter.

Betty stomped across the room, "THEY HAVE A DEAD BODY IN THIS HOUSE? ON PURPOSE?"

"Well," I said. "One of two. Go wash your hands." I pointed to the other three girls. "Go with her."

My eyes didn't leave the guests. Now, with the girls gone, it would be easier to hide a knife. Soo Jin finished Caroline and started on Dennis, who smiled a bit too much for my liking. The others stayed in their line, keeping a close eye on the search and each other.

"I didn't find anything," Soo Jin joined me. "They're all clean."

When she was done, I had Soo Jin recheck the sofas and chairs before allowing everyone to sit down. The room was knife-free. And so were the guests. But what was I going to do? Keep them in here until the storm ended?

And what about Miriam and Ned? They'd have to be searched too. Right now, they were probably in the kitchen, which was knife central. Miriam shouldn't be a problem, but I was betting that Ned wouldn't like being searched. I'd have to do that later, when I'd come up with a decent reason he couldn't argue with.

The girls returned. Betty's hands were bright red from scrubbing, and the other three had stopped laughing. They took up their positions and continued to search the room.

"I need a drink!" Thad got to his feet and headed toward the dining room.

I blocked him. "Stay here."

I sent Stacey and Juliette to get the drinks cart. Stacey had regained some of her composure, but Juliette was glaring at me. I was sure she thought this was my fault and was plotting how to bust me for it. At least she was keeping these thoughts to herself.

"Is this how it's going to be now?" The man sneered. "Who put you in charge, anyway?"

"I did," I snapped back, matching his glare. "Sit down. You can get a drink in a moment."

The cart arrived, and the two women went from person to person, pouring cocktails.

"What if the drinks are poisoned?" Dennis looked at his glass of scotch warily.

"Don't drink it then," I insisted. "It's not like we have a lab where we can test every bottle. You'll have to decide if you want to take that chance."

"The poem doesn't say any more about poison," Wren said hopefully.

She swallowed her glass of wine in one gulp. We all watched her for a moment. If she dropped dead, we'd have to live on water from the tap. When she didn't turn purple and fall to the floor, I figured we were all safe.

The others must've felt the same way, because they took their drinks and downed them, asking for refills. I said nothing. If it mellowed people out and made them relax, that would be a bonus.

"The killer," I mused, "went to all this trouble. He's going to stick to the poem. Which means no matter what, he's going to get his hands on a knife. Do we keep everyone here? I don't think we have the resources to search the entire house."

"How long do you think they'll want to stay here under room arrest?" she asked. "At some point, we have to let people use the bathrooms and eat. We can't keep them here forever."

I nodded. Once again I thought that it would be so much easier if the killer jumped up on the couch and proclaimed himself. But that wasn't going to happen. This murderer wanted to take down seven more victims. And until he did, I was pretty sure he wasn't going to reveal himself.

The afternoon wore on, and the storm continued to batter the house. At one point, the power came back on, which was nice. Things were getting a bit too primitive for me with a houseful of lit candles. And the last thing I wanted was to burn the Deivers' house down. It was bad enough someone was killed here. Leaving them homeless would be terrible.

Stacey asked if she and Juliette could run to the library. I didn't see any harm in it, and possibly a benefit if the killer took out my nemesis. After a few minutes, the women returned with a huge stack of books for people to read. That was an excellent idea, and it gave people a way to pass the time.

Well, not Dennis. He didn't seem to be much of a reader, unless you counted comic books. He just glared at his phone in silence. This seemed like a perfect opportunity to press him to talk about this friend who was writing a book on me. I joined him.

"What do you want?" The words were threatening, but the voice was timid. He was right to be afraid.

"I want to know more about this friend of yours who's writing a book about me."

He narrowed his eyes. "Why is it any of your business?"

My eyes narrowed. "You're joking, right? It's an unauthorized biography about me."

I waited for the words to sink in. It appeared that the guy wasn't just a slacker—but a bit of a nitwit as well. Maybe that was why he was such a flop at life. A sloth had more ambition.

After a few seconds of studying me and perhaps wondering if I was dangerous, he spoke. "She didn't say."

My jaw dropped. "You weren't kidding? Your friend's a she? You're friends with a woman?" Okay, so it probably wasn't smart to say that, but I was caught off guard.

"Yes!" Dennis snapped. "I know women. I have friends who are women!"

I attempted to defuse the situation. "Of course you do. Who is this would-be author?"

He shrugged and went back to looking at his phone.

"I'm not leaving," I levelled at him, "until you tell me. I'll sit here until you give me a name."

"Whatever." He rolled his eyes.

Apparently I wasn't that much of a threat. But I knew who was.

"Girls!" I called out. "Over here!"

Dennis turned an unlikely shade of gray as the girls lined up in front of him.

"Mr. Blunt here"—I smiled—"wants you to sing him every Girl Scout song you know!" I turned to the man. "They know the words to one hundred and thirty-six songs. It'll take two hours to sing them all. I know because I've timed them."

The man began to make a strange, choking sound.

"I think you should start with 'Hermie the Worm,'" I suggested.

Immediately the four girls launched into the song of a worm who grows bigger as he eats larger and more impossible objects. Finally, in the end, the worm burps and goes back to his original size. I always thought it a good metaphor for camp and s'mores. My troop loved making s'mores and often ate the first two they made. However, they never stopped there, figuring that I would eat all they could make when they were full. I once ate fifteen s'mores in thirty minutes. I was Hermie the Worm.

Dennis squirmed uneasily but said nothing. He wasn't going to give up the information if he could help it. And while I was particularly creative when it came to torture, nothing seemed to strike terror in the hearts of men like an old-fashioned, super loud, and off-key Girl Scout singalong.

"After this one"—I leaned toward him—"they know a great song about dirty socks at camp."

The others reacted to the singing. Arthur and Violet smiled warmly, even tapping their toes. Caroline ignored the girls. She'd moved on from staring at every piece of art in the room to staring out the window. Maybe she thought the rain-bombarded window was another abstract painting. Taylor scowled, Thad fumed, and Wren just looked constipated.

"When *I* was a Girl Scout," Taylor said, "*I* knew every single camp song. I got a prize for that!"

The girls ignored her and kept singing.

Dennis looked miserable, but he wasn't giving in.

The song ended to wild applause from the Kasinskis and tepid applause by Wren.

Taylor piped up, "When *I* was a Girl Scout, *I* wrote five songs that are now used internationally."

Man, she was annoying. Maybe I could "accidentally" leave a knife somewhere with a note suggesting Taylor as the next victim. And yes, I knew that was immature and irresponsible…which was why I didn't say it out loud.

Dennis wasn't budging. It was time to bring out the big guns.

"How about an interactive song? I know!" I pulled Betty over, opposite Dennis. "How about 'Wisconsin Milk'?"

This was a song you needed a partner for. You clapped during the song, but at the chorus, you interlaced your fingers, thumbs pointing down, and your partner "milked" your thumbs while you *mooed*. I forced his hands into position, and the song began. The moment Betty "milked" his thumbs, he gave up faster than any terrorist I'd ever "worked with."

Did you know you can waterboard a lactose-intolerant man with Ben and Jerry's? I know, it doesn't sound like torture to me either, but that arms dealer in Tashkent sang like a bird when I plied him with Chunky Monkey.

"Alright! I'll tell you! Make it stop!" he shrieked as he wiggled his hands as if they were on fire.

My girls didn't even look offended. They seemed to know I was using their talents for evil, and they didn't mind one bit.

"Excellent!" Arthur applauded. "Come over here and show me and Violet how to do that!"

Ava, Inez, Lauren, and Betty raced over and began showing the couple how the song worked.

"Well?" I insisted. "Don't make me hurt you. You know I was in the CIA. I can do things with mayonnaise, an Advil, and a pipe cleaner that can cause physical pain."

Dennis did not look happy. "I wasn't supposed to tell you. She said it was a surprise and you'd be happy about it." He squirmed a bit more. "But maybe she was wrong."

I nodded. "*She* was wrong. Who is it?"

"She's really nice. I don't know her last name." He slumped, which was impressive considering he was almost horizontal. "Pretty too."

"You consider a pretty woman whose name you don't know to be a friend?"

"Well, yeah," he hedged. "She asked me out for coffee sometime. We didn't set a date or anything yet."

This was starting to sound like he'd been targeted. It was an old CIA tactic. Find some idiot, promise him some sort of public date, and make him feel better about himself to the point he'd do anything for you, including coughing up information. Nine times out of ten, you never had to follow through with the date.

"Who. Was. It," I said in clipped tones.

"She said…" He licked his lips. "That you knew her. She said her name was Lana."

CHAPTER SIX

You know how sometimes when you hit your thumb with a hammer or eat an insanely hot pepper or hear that a woman who once tried to kill you is writing a book on you, the world freezes and you sort of shrink to a fraction of your size while everything gets weirdly quiet?

"Lana?" I squeaked. "What did she look like?"

He went on to describe a woman I knew as an ex-Russian spy. A woman who, a few months back, had been allegedly traded back to Russia. A woman I'd sworn I'd seen recently.

She was in Iowa! I knew it! And she was tormenting me by making me deal with a sniveling man-brat who claimed she was writing a book about me. The good news was that it was doubtful she was actually writing a book. The woman was in deep hiding. If the Feds found her, she was headed straight to the nearest maximum-security prison. Trying to sell a book about anything would end with her return to jail.

My thoughts were interrupted by a loud scream. I jumped up to see my girls and the rest of the guests pulling one of the couches away from the wall. All concerns about Lana went out the window.

"What is it?" I ran over to see. "Is it a knife?"

Lauren pointed to a large, perfectly rounded hole in the wall, just above the floor. It looked like a cartoon mouse hole, if the mouse was the size of a bobcat.

"Gertrude! We saw Gertrude!" Inez jumped up and down.

"She's so cute!" Ava swooned. "She had a piece of paper in her mouth and was nibbling on it!"

I bent to examine the hole. I didn't know anything about lop-eared bunnies. But how different could they be from cats? I reached in and heard something skitter away. Yup. She was in there alright.

"Do you think she has holes like that in every room?" Betty asked.

"I don't know." This was a new development. "But she's gone now." I got to my feet.

"Can we go look in the other rooms?" Lauren pleaded, surrounded by three little girls who were also begging.

"No. Sorry," I answered. "If she popped in, she might do it again. We'll just have to watch out for her. But right now, Gertrude isn't our biggest priority."

"How is that adorable rabbit not our biggest priority?" Lauren's eyes grew wide, like saucers. But I wasn't falling for that trap, like I usually did, 99.9 percent of the time.

"Yeah," Betty spoke up. "What's more important than a cute, cuddly bunny?"

"Well, murder, for one." I helped shove the couch back into place. "We have to stay together. There's safety in numbers."

Inez shook her head. "Then we need to keep Gertrude safe!"

I looked at the size of the hole. "She's much safer in the walls than out here with us. Trust me."

Soo Jin stepped up with my favorite tactic with the girls—distraction. Quietly she drew the girls over to one corner of the room, where she tied them into a human knot.

It's not what it sounds like. Okay, it is, but it's a team-building game and something we use as a distraction whenever we need to. Like now.

The girls all get into a close circle. One puts her right hand out and grabs the hand of a girl opposite her. Then with her left hand, she grasps the hand of another girl. This goes on until each girl is holding hands with two other girls. At that point, you have a human knot. And the girls have to twist and bend to untangle themselves, without letting go, until they are standing in a straight line.

It could take minutes or hours. Usually it took hours. Which made it my favorite activity. I'd gotten a lot done during the human knot, from cooking over a fire to setting up the archery range to cutting twenty pieces of bubblegum out of a Kaitlyn's hair after an unfortunate bubble-blowing competition.

Things settled down in the room as everyone watched the girls work to free themselves. The Human Knot turned out to be a welcome distraction for the adults too. A clap of thunder and the room blazed from the flash of a lightning bolt outside the window. The storm gave no sign of letting up. Soon we'd have to think about dinner, which made me wonder where Miriam and Ned were.

There was a quick scream, and I turned to see if Gertrude had made her way back here. Instead, I saw that Wren was pale and pointing at the table with the clay figures. A second misshapen animal was down and broken into two pieces.

"Who's messing with us?" she threatened. "This isn't funny!"

My throat constricted as I counted the people in the room. We were short one person. Taylor Burke was gone.

"Where's Taylor?" I demanded.

That was when the others noticed she was gone too.

"She was just here." Thad frowned, even looking a bit worried.

Caroline spoke up. "Said she had to use the bathroom."

Soo Jin chastised her. "You let her go alone?"

The gastroenterologist shrugged. "She said she'd be fine since the murderer was in here."

"Everyone stay put," I ordered. "I'm going to look for her."

Soo Jin shook her head. "Not without me."

The two of us walked out into the hall. The others followed us to the doorway but stayed put. The bathroom door under the staircase was open. I peeked in, but the Insurance CEO of the Year wasn't there.

We walked past the hall and looked into the entryway, but it too was empty.

"Taylor?" I shouted. There was no answer.

Soo Jin led the way across to the study, and I followed. As she went into the room, the medical examiner hesitated for a split second before bolting inside. I chased after to find her kneeling beside the body of Taylor Burke.

"Is she…" I asked.

Soo Jin nodded. "Dead. Stabbed."

"But we didn't find a knife on anyone," I said as I walked around her.

"The killer didn't need one," the doctor said.

Taylor lay on the floor, looking as though she'd just fallen asleep, except for the fact that she had some sort of trophy plunged into the side of her neck.

Victim number two had fallen to the poem.

"What is it?" Stacey called from outside the room. From the tone in her voice, I could tell that she'd rather not know the answer.

"We have to tell them," Soo Jin said.

"How did it happen?" I asked.

She nodded. "Stabbed in the jugular vein. She probably couldn't speak. Died in seconds."

"Enos wasn't a one-off," I murmured.

Soo Jin agreed. "No, Enos wasn't a one-off. We're dealing with multiple murders here."

"How could this happen? We'd frisked everyone and kept an eye on things!"

Except for when Gertrude made an appearance. Was the bunny working with Kevin the Killer? And before you think I'm ridiculous, it does happen. I once knew a guy in Italy who trained his donkey to bite people while he *liberated* their wallets and purses. If he hadn't been one of my best informants, I might have said something to him about it.

I joined Stacey in the doorway and filled her in while asking her to keep the others at bay. She took people back to the lounge to explain that the killer had struck again, as Soo Jin examined the body. First, Enos died in the dining room. Now, Taylor was murdered in the study. If only I'd brought crime tape! I'd wanted to, but my Hitler look-alike cat, Philby, got into it, rolling in the thin plastic tape until the static made it stick to her like a mummy. Rex promised to have her untangled before I got back.

Rex! If only I could get ahold of him somehow. He'd rather be here dealing with this, I knew. Unfortunately, he was back home in Who's There, completely unaware that I was now dealing with multiple murders.

What would my detective husband make of this if he were here? First, he'd roll his eyes because I was, yet again, involved in a murder. Which was kind of unfair, since I had nothing to do with what was going on here.

Still, what would he do first? Close off the scene, look for clues, and call the medical examiner. Hey! We were doing that! I didn't even have to wait for Dr. Body because she was on the scene! Would he give me credit for running this investigation like he would?

You know, it hadn't escaped my notice that, with the exception of a pizza delivery guy in his driveway, this never happened to him. And as soon as I was back in his arms and out of here, I'd tell him that. In the meantime, Soo Jin and I had to make do with what we had, which was two dead people and a poem about killing Girl Scouts. Not a lot to go on.

"Did you find anything?" I asked the medical examiner as I faced the hallway.

The others didn't seem too eager to want to see the body, which was good. The girls, however, were trying to break free from Stacey's and Juliette's grasps. I was pretty sure they wanted to be on the scene. This was a little too horrific, even for them.

"Nothing." Soo Jin sighed. "Not so much as a scrap of fabric. There aren't even any defensive injuries. Taylor never knew what hit her."

"Or…" I turned toward her. "She felt safe with whoever it was."

My thoughts turned to Thad. What if the two of them had slipped away for a little secret canoodling? They'd seemed pretty cozy this whole time. Had Thad killed her as a way to get out of the affair? That seemed a little drastic to me.

Unfortunately, we'd all been distracted by Gertrude. Maybe Wren had followed her out of the room unnoticed and killed her? Or maybe Juliette was fed up with all the annoying

When I was in Girl Scouts...blah, blah, blah and took her out. If so, I couldn't really blame her for that.

"How much force would it have taken to kill her?" I asked Dr. Body quietly.

She looked thoughtful. "It's not so much force as surprise. Look at this."

I held up my hands to Stacey to indicate she was to stay out there. The terrified woman agreed.

Soo Jin had removed the trophy and covered the woman with an afghan. Using a piece of cloth, she held up the weapon. It was a huge gold fencing trophy with a rather large and pointy rapier. I looked around the room.

"Why use this?" I asked, motioning around me. "There are ink pens and a letter opener on the desk. Wouldn't they have worked better?"

"Yes. Definitely. Using the trophy was a gamble because the base is so heavy," she said. "It would've been hard to aim to get it in the right spot."

"The killer is trying to tell us something."

Using the same cloth, I took the trophy from her. There was a large plaque that read, *Winner of the Grand Prix*. Why use a trophy instead of a knife? Even though we searched people, it would've been easier to smuggle one in instead of using this trophy.

"I'm guessing it came from here." Soo Jin pointed to a circular mark on a dusty shelf. "It was owned by the Deivers."

"Only they aren't here, so we know it isn't them," I added.

I called out for Stacey and Juliette to fetch a large plastic bag, and they did so with great speed. Once the trophy was in the bag, I turned it around looking for clues but found nothing.

"Basement?" Soo Jin asked.

That was when I noticed she'd rolled the body up in the rug it had been lying on, securing it with decorative ropes from the drapes.

"Yes." I sighed. "But this time we're getting some help."

Neither Thad nor Dennis wanted any part of moving Taylor to the basement. I didn't give them an option. Once I'd explained what had happened, a malaise of depression settled over the group. As Stacey herded everyone into the dining room, I'd pulled the two men aside and forcibly drafted them into service.

The men worked wordlessly. I couldn't get a read on Thad's expression. Was he upset? Guilty? It was impossible to tell from the scowl on his face. They placed the body next to Enos and ran up the stairs to join the rest of us.

"How did this happen?" Wren wailed. If she was Taylor's killer, she was doing a great job hiding the fact.

"*Why* is this happening?" Violet sobbed as Arthur wrapped her into his arms. He looked devastated.

Dennis sat at the table, his face buried in his hands. Thad glared at the rest of us, like he'd been doing since he arrived. Caroline's face was unreadable, but then, she always looked like that.

Stacey paced, and Juliette scowled. The girls sat at their little table, talking quietly, looking at the guests from time to time. No one seemed eager to leave the room. They were all in shock and happy to take orders from me. I was afraid to leave the group alone, but it seemed that the killer was picking his victims off one at a time. It was unlikely he would burst in and mow everyone down with a machine gun.

No. Kevin the Killer had taken the time to create a poem predicting how each person would die. I couldn't see him changing his modus operandi. He was confident that we had no idea who he was. All we knew was who he wasn't—Taylor or Enos. However, at this rate, we'd be running out of suspects soon, as he took out his victims one at a time. And that was when he'd be at his most dangerous—when he was closest to discovery.

No matter what it took, I couldn't let that happen. These people were annoying and in some cases horrible, but they didn't deserve to die. We had to be more vigilant. We had to keep everyone together until this was over. I wasn't sure how Soo Jin and I were going to do that, but we had to try. But first we had to do something about dinner. Even if they didn't feel like it, people needed to eat. To keep their strength up. And while we were eating, I'd come up with some sort of brilliant plan.

Soo Jin and I went to the kitchen to find Ned and Miriam, but they weren't there. We continued to search the ground floor, but the staff was nowhere to be found. Were they the killers? They certainly moved around freely enough. Or had they retreated to their cottage, where they knew they'd be safe?

My stomach rumbled. When you work in espionage, you get a cast-iron gut. Very little will stop me from eating. I wasn't worried about Soo Jin—this was her job. If working with the dead made her lose her appetite, she'd starve to death. It was the others I was worried about. Miriam would have to make something amazing to get these guys to eat. But first we had to find her.

The cottage was behind the house, so we decided to go outside and, staying on the wraparound porch, see if we could find them. The storm was just as intense as it had been all day, but we held on to the railing and made our way to the back of the house as the rain slapped us around.

The cottage was a three-room building laid out like a very small ranch house behind the main house. From the porch we could see lights on inside, but the land between the two buildings had flooded into a deep, muddy trench.

For about five minutes we shouted at the cottage, but the wind killed any sound as soon as it escaped our lips.

"This is not working!" I shouted to Soo Jin, who was standing right next to me.

"Let's go back in!" she called out.

In spite of being on the covered porch, we were pretty much soaked when we made it back inside. I threw the deadbolt.

We entered the dining room. With the exception of the girls, the expressions we saw were grim and fearful. And it was getting late. What little sun we'd had was vanishing as we moved toward evening.

"Is anyone hungry?" I asked.

There was no reply.

"Hold on for a minute. Soo Jin and I need to go change out of our wet clothes. Okay?"

The girls nodded, but they were the only ones.

"I'm going to my room." Thad stood up. "I'm tired of sitting around doing nothing."

That was just what I'd expect from the murderer. Was he not afraid of splitting up because he knew he was the killer?

"I agree," said Caroline. "I'll be safer in my locked room than here."

It wasn't long before everyone seemed to think this was a good idea, including Soo Jin and myself since we were all wet. I knew the time would come when the adults would insist on doing what they wanted. They weren't little girls. We couldn't make them stay together.

"Okay," I said. "Head to your rooms. Lock your doors. If anyone's hungry in an hour, join us in the dining room." The bit in the poem about drowning popped into my mind. "And don't take a bath or run water in the sink. Just…just stay dry."

Maybe I should've said I'd check on them, room by room, but I got the distinct impression that no one wanted this. In fact, I was starting to think that my leadership was resented.

Soo Jin led the way up the stairs, the girls behind her with me bringing up the rear. Once inside, I bolted the door and we changed into dry clothes. I sat down on my bed and noticed that the girls were sitting on the floor with a board game.

"What are you guys playing?" I tried to sound cheerful. The idea of them having a little fun seemed like a good idea, considering that this was quickly turning into a murder house.

"Clue," Betty said without looking up.

I joined the girls on the floor. I'd loved that game when I was a kid. Of course, now we were playing it for real…

"Hey!" I snatched up the game board. "The house on the board looks just like this house!"

It was true. The layout of the board was the exact same layout as this house! That was why it seemed so familiar.

"That's strange." Soo Jin joined us. "It is. It's exactly the same." She jumped up and grabbed the book on Iowa islands in lakes from her bed. "This house was built in the 1880s by Jim and June Bentley." She showed us a picture of the architectural plans.

"That has to be before the game came out." I stared at it. "What are the odds?"

A clap of thunder was followed by a bolt of lightning that lit up the room. This was followed by an even louder *boom* that seemed to shake the house.

The girls, for the first time all day, looked nervous.

"I'm going to get you guys out of here safe and sound," I promised.

Lauren took the Clue board and propped it up on the dresser. "Right. Let's see what we can do to catch this killer. This is our murder board."

"We need people." Betty examined the game. "So we can put the bodies in the rooms where they were found."

I rifled through a desk in the room and found some Post-its. Inez, the artist in the group, cut little figures out and put one in the dining room and another in the study.

She was very creative. Enos was fat and had *X*'s for eyes and a fish in his stomach. She knew Taylor had been stabbed in the neck, so she made a giant knife sticking out of her throat. I didn't correct her.

"Can you make figures for the rest of us?" Soo Jin asked as she studied the board.

The whole troop got in on this action, with Inez cutting out the figures and the rest of them decorating everyone. I was a little taken aback that I had a unicorn horn and body and Soo Jin looked like a princess with a formal gown and long hair, but I decided not to interrupt the creative flow.

Betty found tape and taped the poem to the board.

"Someone is going to drown next," she said.

"Hopefully not." I chewed my lip as I studied the board. When Taylor was murdered, everyone but the two victims had been in the lounge. "Did you see anyone else leave the room besides Taylor?"

The girls and Soo Jin shook their heads.

"We were trying to grab Gertrude," Ava announced.

"Did anyone see Taylor leave?" I asked.

Everyone shook their heads. Dr. Caroline Regent seemed to be the only one who'd known Taylor was leaving, but she didn't mention anyone else. Someone might have seen something. But why keep it to themselves? Was it out of fear that the killer would turn on them?

"There's no second floor or basement," Soo Jin said.

"We can draw one," I said, pointing to the girls. "One of you make a mockup of this floor, and someone else do the basement."

Betty shrugged. "We don't know what the basement looks like."

Lauren agreed. "We should go down there. That would give us a chance to examine the bodies."

I shook my head. "No one is going to examine the bodies. The basement is just one large, open square. There's nothing down there. Draw that."

The girls grumbled but did it. They also drew little stick figure bodies with *X*'s over their eyes. Lauren ran to her bag, returning with clay.

"We can create 3-D reenactments of each scene! Like who was sitting where at the table when Enos was killed!"

Ava nodded. "And where everyone was sitting in the lounge when Taylor was stabbed!"

"That"—Soo Jin beamed—"is an excellent idea! Very clever of you girls!"

When the beyond-beautiful Korean-American doctor smiled at you, you felt like you were wrapped in a warm blanket. I'm not kidding, because on occasion I've fallen for her charms. I wasn't completely sure she was aware of this, but at the hospital, she left a wake of smitten men and women when she was in a good mood—which was always.

The girls worked quickly, creating little clay people that technically looked like giraffes. They added little features, like Enos brushing his teeth at the table and Taylor with a sword sticking out of her neck. I regretted telling them how she died.

The first diorama featured the dining room. Two small pieces of cardboard made up the adult and kiddie tables. Each character kind of stood around the cardboard. They didn't have legs, just a lump of clay. Maybe that was the chair.

I leaned in to study the piece as they moved on to recreate Taylor's murder. In the dining room, Enos and Thad had been at opposite ends of the table, and the seating was mostly boy-girl. Caroline and Violet sat on either side of Enos. Dennis sat between Caroline and Taylor, while Arthur sat between his wife and Wren. That was when the boy-girl thing fell apart, because Stacey and Juliette sat between Wren and Thad, and Soo Jin and I were on his other side.

The girls sat at their table, as much larger figures than the rest of us. What was that? Each girl seemed to be armed with a weapon from the game. Well, they weren't armed as much as the little plastic candlestick, dagger, pistol, and so on were sort of squished into the clay figures' heads. Why were they armed?

"Hey," I mumbled as I pointed to two misshapen lumps on my figure's head. "What's this?"

Ava shrugged. "Rhino horns. I thought you needed them."

"Why do I need rhino horns?" I picked up the figure. It looked more like a couple of roundish blobs.

Inez looked at the others before rolling her eyes at me. "Because! Rhino horns make you awesome!" The other girls nodded, indicating that no further explanation was needed.

Soo Jin's clay figure was perfectly rendered. She was almost professionally sculpted with the perfect body, long legs, and big eyes. I guessed she was awesome enough and didn't need horns like I did. The rest of the guests looked more like me, except for Miriam, who was ridiculously small, and Ned, who was rendered a giant with huge, scary teeth.

I forced my thoughts toward the dining room scene. Did it matter where people sat? Attention was drawn to Thad when Enos died. No one had seen anything until one of my girls announced Enos's death. Could Caroline have put something in Enos's lunch? She was a doctor and the most likely to have access to cyanide. But that wouldn't work because Enos would've noticed that since he was probably facing front, looking at Thad with the rest of us. The poison must've been added in the kitchen or when the plate was en route to the table. And only Miriam and Ned handled the dishes.

The other scene was in two rooms. Taylor lay dead on the floor in the study, while the rest of us were staring at a wall in the lounge, surrounding what might have been Gertrude, except that the rabbit was the size of a horse.

"Is this where everyone was?" I asked.

As I recalled, I was over by the wall, studying the hole behind Gertrude. The girls had been with me, crowded around the big bunny. It was so weird that a mini lop would be large. But Mrs. Deivers had assured me the name was misleading. I wondered if…oh geez. *Focus, Merry!*

At the time, everyone else had been leaning toward us. It was such a tight group, I couldn't figure out how the killer could've slipped away and murdered Taylor without notice.

"Okay," Betty announced. "This is how the murders happened."

"Except for Kevin the Killer," Lauren said as she plopped a ghoulish-looking blob with a skull for a head behind Enos while he was seated.

Ava had Kevin sneaking up on Enos, before shoving him face down on the table. The Killer was then moved to the lounge mockup, where it tiptoed to the study and made a sort of stabby movement toward Taylor. Then he moved back to the lounge.

"As you can see," Inez said, "the killer could be anyone." She sat down, and the others congratulated themselves for not solving anything.

We were no closer to the truth.

Soo Jin looked at her watch. "An hour is up. We said we'd be downstairs in the dining room for dinner."

She was right. Even if no one else joined us, we were going to eat. Besides, Miriam and Ned might be there, setting the table for dinner. They hadn't been around when Taylor was killed, and I wanted to tell them so I could study their reactions. The two of them were an interesting case. Both worked and lived here. It was unlikely that they knew the guests. But did it rule them out as killers? And if they worked together, would it be Kevin and Kate the Killers? They were the only ones not in the lounge with the rest of us.

I got to my feet. "Okay, let's go."

We returned to the dining room the way we came up—Soo Jin in the lead, the girls in the middle, and me bringing up the rear. The girls took their seats at the kids' table in the corner.

The table had been set for dinner, and we could hear Miriam and Ned clanking dishes and murmuring in the kitchen.

The remaining guests trickled in quietly. The idea of dinner seemed to relax them a little because it was routine. As they took their seats, I told Stacey and Juliette to watch things, noting anyone coming or going, so Soo Jin and I could head to the kitchen.

Miriam was pulling a tray of Cornish hens from the oven while Ned opened several bottles of wine. The aroma of roasted meat overwhelmed my senses, and I almost forgot why I was there.

"Where have you been?" I asked, once I remembered.

The two looked at each other. Ned scowled. "At the cottage. Why?"

Soo Jin filled them in on Taylor's murder, and I studied their responses. Miriam's eyes flew open wide, and she started trembling. Ned frowned and started to pace.

"We didn't do it!" he said at last. "You don't think we did it, do you?"

Honestly? I had no idea. My instincts were taking a nap. I couldn't get a read. The fact that they weren't with the rest of us in the lounge when it happened meant they certainly could've killed Taylor.

"I don't know who did it," I said. "But stick together. Don't go anywhere alone. Okay?"

They nodded and went back to work. Ned patted Miriam on the back awkwardly. She really seemed stricken. But was that because she was shocked or because she was afraid she was going to get caught? For a moment I hesitated, wondering what else I could do to get a confession out of them. Unfortunately, I came up blank.

As Soo Jin and I returned to the dining room, I informed the guests of the menu and sat down. We were all seated when the food came in. Steaming plates of seasoned meat with finger potatoes and asparagus distracted us from the deadly events of the afternoon. The question was, would everyone eat?

I'd never had dinner with a killer before, but I assumed that they'd eat ravenously, while the others hesitated. It seemed important to study everyone to see if this was true.

The girls were given hot dogs and french fries, much to their approval. But this time I let them be. The Cornish hens were golden brown and juicy, and for once I was glad to be at the adult table.

Ned poured the wine, and I noticed a few of the guests staring at their glasses. The next murder would be drowning, but I was pretty sure it wasn't going to happen in a wineglass. Besides, the last murder took place in another room. I didn't think the killer would be as brazen as they were with Enos.

My thoughts turned to the idea of drowning. Technically speaking, you can drown in a few inches of water. The bathtubs, sinks, and even toilets were possibilities. But then, so was the huge lake that surrounded the island.

Would the killer risk taking someone out to the lake? The storm hadn't let up, and they seemed to want each body discovered. We might not find someone who drowned in a lake until this was over.

I took a sip of wine, and when I didn't spasm and die, the others relaxed and reached for their glasses. That was a relief. People can be unpredictable—even more so if they're terrified and panicking. While this was a horrific situation, having cool heads would go a long way in getting us out alive.

So, what was the plan? Staying together seemed smart, but Taylor's murder showed the flaws in that idea. Had she thought that she was safe slipping away since the killer would be with everyone else? I wasn't ruling out a secret liaison with Thad.

Another idea struck. Maybe the killer wasn't one of us? Could he be someone we didn't know about? Someone hiding out here, striking when opportunity presented itself? Kevin the Killer could've poisoned Enos's food in the kitchen when Miriam and Ned were serving. But how would they know which plate he'd get?

Which led back to the idea that this was a random killer who didn't care who he murdered, as long as it followed the poem. In fact, I was the only victim specifically mentioned, unless someone else had been in the CIA, which I sincerely doubted. I was pretty sure I was listed as the last victim on purpose, but the rest of the murders in the poem could be anyone else.

I liked it better when I thought it was more organized than that.

"What are you doing about this?" Thad was glaring at me.

"Everything I can," I answered with as much authority as I could muster. "Dr. Body here has police training. Together we will try to stop these murders from happening and find out who's behind it all."

Did the guests buy that?

"Why"—Thad pointed with his fork at Stacey and Juliette—"aren't they in charge?"

The two Girl Scout employees looked at each other and then turned to me. Which answered Thad's question.

"Mrs. Wrath's husband is a detective!" Betty stood and shouted. "And she's solved murders before!"

The other girls stood, folded their arms over their chests, and nodded. My posse.

"Look." I set my knife and fork down. "I don't want to be in charge. I'd rather let someone else take over. Go ahead and volunteer if you like. But you have to use Dr. Body's skills."

It grew very quiet. Dennis looked at Caroline and Thad. Wren plucked at her husband's sleeve, and Arthur put his arm around Violet before looking at me and nodding.

"I think Mrs. Wrath should be in charge," the elderly man said. "But I am worried about the children. We need to do everything we can to keep them safe."

I loved him in that moment.

Violet nodded. "The poem is about Girl Scouts. I'm afraid they may be targets."

The Kasinskis were selfless. Arthur was a large man, even if he was elderly, and I knew I could count on him in a pinch. He'd spent most of his life dragging pigs around, so in spite of his age, he was probably fairly strong should I need help subduing anyone. The question was, could I count on the others?

"Okay," Caroline said glumly before going back to her dinner.

Dennis gave a wordless nod and drained his wineglass in one gulp.

"Fine!" Thad snapped. Wren added her agreement with a little nod.

I made a silent prayer that no one would die at dinner. The Cornish hens were amazing, and I wanted to at least eat a whole meal. It's selfish, I know, but if I was supposed to be in charge here, the least the killer could do was let me eat.

"I have a question," I said as the others continued eating. "Did anyone see someone other than Taylor leave the room?"

They all thought about this and shook their heads. I wasn't sure what I expected. Surely anyone who saw the killer leave would've said something by now. Still, it felt important to put the question out there.

"Do you think"—Wren's voice shook—"that it's the staff?" She peeked nervously at the doorway.

Soo Jin spoke up. "Everyone here is a suspect until we prove otherwise."

That started an uproar. Everyone but the Kasinskis sputtered defensively, each insisting that they weren't the killer. Thad made mention of suing me for slander, while Caroline muttered that I'd better never need a bowel surgeon. I made a mental note to add more fiber to my diet, just in case.

"I think you're right," Arthur said at last.

Thad sneered. "I noticed that you didn't insist it wasn't you or your wife."

"Thad!" Wren squeaked. "The Kasinskis would never do something like this!"

"No, no," Arthur eased. "It's fair to ask. I just didn't think I needed to add to the complaining." He set his fork down and made eye contact with Thad. "Someone here is doing this. We have to keep calm and figure it out before there's another victim."

I really, really loved him.

"The fact is," he continued, "we need to look after one another and keep an eye out for anything unusual."

Thad stood up and threw down his napkin in disgust. "Well, I'd say these murders are pretty damned unusual!"

Was Thad upset that his lover had been killed or worried that he might be a target? Sadly for Taylor, my money was on the latter. His fear sounded genuine. But did that mean he wasn't the killer? I wasn't ready to take him off the suspect list just yet.

Arthur regarded the younger man. "You're absolutely right. But getting hysterical is not going to help."

"That's very true," Violet agreed with her husband. "We are all adults here. Let's act like it."

Wren tugged on Thad's sleeve until he sat back down. He looked angry and defeated all at once.

"I don't want to die," Dennis grumbled. "Unlike the old people here, I haven't lived my life."

"Like you live at all!" Thad snapped. "You're just a slacker. You don't contribute to society like the rest of us!"

Okay, to be fair, I'd also been thinking what Thad said—I just didn't think it was fair to say it out loud. And I wasn't happy about his dig at Arthur and Violet. What was wrong with this guy?

"What contribution?" Dennis roared. "You defend the scum of the earth! And I have something to contribute!"

"Oh yeah?" Thad's voice dripped with sarcasm. "And what's that?"

Dennis frowned. Apparently he had no idea what he had to offer. "My parents' money! When they die, I'll have that!"

Okay… Not exactly the *best* answer…

Thad got to his feet and threw his napkin on the table. "That doesn't help your case. You'll just turn their house into a juvenile man cave and won't need to change your sweats as often!"

Nobody really knew how to respond to that, including Dennis, who remained silent.

"Sit DOWN!" Juliette thundered. "This is not the time for personal attacks!"

That seemed hypocritical, coming from a woman who had done nothing but launch one personal attack on me after another. It was kind of nice to see her aim her venom at someone else for a change.

"Juliette is right." Stacey placed a hand on her colleague's arm. "And so is Mrs. Kasinski. We need to act like adults. Yelling at each other will only help the killer."

Juliette nodded and sat back down, and after a second of stomping his feet and growling, Thad did too.

"Death," Caroline said without emotion, "is just another part of life."

The others looked at her with shock in their eyes. The doctor looked up and realized she'd said something scandalous and shrugged.

"It's true. People die all the time."

I looked at Soo Jin and my girls. Not them. They weren't going to die anytime soon while I had breath in my body.

A skittering sound drew all attention to the doorway, where a huge white lop-eared bunny stopped and looked us all over. Her nose twitched, and her right ear was raised, crookedly, toward us.

Gertrude took a tentative hop into the room. She probably wondered who all these strangers were. She rose to a standing position, sniffing the air. Then she rubbed her front paws all over her face, as if just moving across the floor had made her filthy. It was ridiculously adorable and a nice distraction.

"She's so cute!" Ava said breathlessly.

"Don't frighten her," I cautioned.

Betty held a french fry out to the rabbit, who slowly hopped over and sniffed it. To my complete surprise, this time, not a single girl lunged for her. Lauren dropped her right hand to her side and wiggled her fingers.

Gertrude hopped over and rubbed the underside of her chin on the girl's fingers before headbutting them. Lauren rubbed the spot between her eyes, and the bunny kicked her hind feet out behind her and sprawled onto the floor. This rabbit had hypnotized the whole room. I wondered if they'd let me borrow her for meetings.

"How did you know to do that?" Soo Jin asked the girl.

"My cousin has a rabbit," Lauren explained. "I think Gertrude likes people."

Great. Now I had a bunny to protect too.

After a few seconds, the rabbit jumped up and ran back and forth, jumping and spinning in the air.

"She's binkying," Lauren said. "When they're happy, they binky."

At least someone was having a good time.

"Who cares about a stupid rodent?" Thad shouted.

Gertrude froze at the outburst then raced out of the room. In seconds we could hear her scuttling inside the walls. It was a dangerous mistake on Thad's part, as four little girls turned toward him with fury in their eyes.

"That was not nice!" Lauren narrowed her eyes at the man.

"What did Gertrude ever do to you?" Ava added.

Betty rolled her eyes. "Someone woke up on the wrong side of murder…"

"Maybe"—Dennis pointed a stubby figure at the attorney—"you're angry because you're the killer."

Thad roared, "You want to say that again, slacker?"

Here we go again.

Dennis nodded. "Yeah. I think you killed Taylor. It's obvious you two were having a fling."

The color drained out of Wren's face, but she didn't defend her husband. And he didn't seem upset at the mention of a possible affair.

"I didn't kill Taylor!" Thad roared. "But if I *was* the killer, you'd be next!"

Dennis puffed out his chest, which was difficult considering he couldn't expand it past his belly.

"STOP IT! RIGHT NOW!" Stacey commanded.

Everyone was so startled by the outburst, the room went silent. Where had this version of the perpetually sweet and optimistic woman come from? I liked it!

"Look!" She glared at the two men. "Like it or not, we're here and we have to deal with this problem. If you're going to exacerbate it and make things worse, you can take your chances outside!"

Juliette's jaw dropped. I guess this was the first time she'd seen her colleague act like this. When it came to the Girl Scouts, Juliette was usually shrieking at me, and yet during this whole event, she didn't say one word. Maybe when I married

Rex, she gave up on hating me? Or, she was taking her time, plotting my demise.

"Now." Stacey sat back down. "Let's finish dinner, and then we can go to the ballroom and discuss our next steps." She flashed a weak grin at my troop. "After all, we have to set an example for the children, and we can't do that by acting like children ourselves."

Arthur clinked his spoon on his water glass. "Yes! She's right. Let's eat in peace for a change."

Dennis and Thad grudgingly picked at their food. I finished every bite on my plate. In these situations, you needed to eat when you could because you never knew when you'd get the chance again.

This was an instinct from my old days as a spy. Whenever the opportunity presented itself, whether it was a banana split or bug kabobs (not bad with teriyaki sauce), I ate. On one of my first assignments, I was following a target as she moved from place to place all over Moscow. She never stopped to eat in twenty hours, and I had no food with me. I almost ate the vinyl seats in the crappy Soviet-era car I'd stolen.

Thank God she finally stopped at an Italian restaurant to have dinner. I probably would've killed her if she hadn't. Alright, to be honest, I did kill her. But much, much later and for something completely legit.

Miriam and Ned appeared to collect the plates, and I noticed Soo Jin watching the others to see if they'd been poisoned. Since no one fell head first into their water glass, she relaxed a little. Especially when the staff returned with cheesecake.

I have a special weakness for cheesecake. Throughout my whole life, I've dropped anything I was doing if a slice appeared near me. I've eaten cheesecakes in Paris, Tashkent, and Bogota. And I've never had a bad one.

"What is that?" Inez made a face.

"Cheesecake," I said. "You'll like it."

Betty's eyes grew round. "They made a cake out of stinky cheese?"

I shook my head. "No. It's cream cheese. Trust me. Try it."

Miriam set a piece in front of Lauren, with strawberries and whipped cream on top. The girl shrugged and took a bite. The other girls watched her carefully, studying her expression. When she smiled, they each took a bite.

"Not bad!" Ava said.

The girls settled. I turned to my piece and savored each and every bite. Things were looking up. No one had died during dinner, and we had cheesecake.

Soo Jin leaned over and whispered, "What are we going to do after dinner?"

BOOM!

A tremendous thunderclap rocked the house, and the power flickered. I prayed silently that it wouldn't go off again. How did this storm manage to continue since noon? At least we had power…for the moment.

Besides the dining room and lounge, the ballroom was a large room where we could get our bearings and figure out what to do next. The conservatory, billiard room, and library were small and would be crowded.

"Shall we head to the ballroom?" I asked the group.

Dishes were shoved aside, and people rose to their feet. Violet was struggling a little, and Lauren and Ava ran to help her. Each girl took an arm and escorted the old woman from the room, much to her and Arthur's delight.

The ballroom had chairs, and we put them together in a circle. The wind picked up, howling outside and rattling branches that scraped the window. Soo Jin and I invited (or rather, insisted) Miriam and Ned. They came grudgingly.

"It looks like," I said once everyone was seated, "we're going to be spending the night here."

I looked at my watch—it was nine o'clock. Arthur and Violet were drooping. Their bedtime was probably soon. Wearing them out wasn't a good idea.

"You don't think the storm will quit and we can leave the island?" Wren asked.

"I honestly don't know." I rubbed my face. "But we can't stay up all night."

"Maybe the killer is done?" Violet suggested. "I think Arthur and I will be alright in our room. With the door locked."

I couldn't tell adults what to do if they wanted to leave. "Anyone who wants to go to bed should. You all know where my room is. If you need help in the night, come find me."

I looked at Ned hopefully. "Maybe you could volunteer to sit in the hallway? I could help."

The man snarled. "I'm going to my room in the cottage. So is Miriam." And with that, the two staff members left the room and presumably the house.

"I'll sit up with you," Stacey said. "Juliette and Dr. Body could relieve us halfway through the night?"

Wren nudged her husband, but he ignored it.

Soo Jin nodded, and I was grateful that she was going to be with Juliette. The idea had merit—it meant one of us would be with our girls the whole night. They were my main priority. I had to keep them safe.

"Anyone who wants to go to bed should. I'll meet Stacey in the hallway in twenty minutes. At three a.m., Dr. Body and Juliette will take over. At eight, we can all meet in the dining room."

Everyone agreed and headed upstairs. I stayed behind, running through the whole house, locking the windows. Soo Jin and the girls waited on the stairs for me, but I wasn't worried about being killed. I was the last person in the poem. We had a ways to go. It was far more important to make sure we were locked up tight.

"I think Thad is the killer," Betty announced as we got settled in our room.

"My money is on Dr. Regent," Lauren said.

"I think it's the old people," Ava said, and Inez agreed.

Soo Jin and I stared at the board. "Alright," I said. "Give me your reasons."

Betty shrugged. "Thad had a motive, right? For Taylor. Because they were boyfriend and girlfriend. And maybe his wife is covering for him."

"Yes." Lauren spoke up. "But Caroline was the only one who saw Taylor go out. She could've followed her out."

Betty argued, "Thad isn't going to tell us he met Taylor in the study."

"Those are very good arguments," Soo Jin said. "But what about Enos? Why would Thad or Caroline kill him?"

"Dennis killed him because he wasn't able to invest in his app," I mused.

"Maybe we have two different murders for two different reasons?" Inez asked.

I turned to Ava. "Why do you think the Kasinskis are the killers?"

Ava shrugged. "They are the least likely so the most obvious. Duh."

It kind of made sense, in a weird way.

"The fact is, you could all be right." I sighed.

"Or the killer is killing off multiple people randomly," Soo Jin said.

"Or he's killing off several people, but only one is the real target," Betty added. "The rest are red herrings."

Inez cocked her head to one side. "What's a red herring?"

Lauren nodded. "It's a red fish."

Ava threw her arms in the air. "Well, what does that have to do with anything?"

"Because the color red means *stop*," Betty said.

The others seemed to agree that this made sense.

"A red herring is an idea that fools you into following it, then it just leads to a dead end. It's meant to confuse you—take you off the trail of the real killer," I explained.

Everyone was mulling this over. I was wondering about our next step. I needed to talk to Wren—get her alone and ask if Thad left the room when Taylor did. But how to approach it? I guess delicacy was thrown out the window when Dennis announced the idea of an affair.

Wren had to know about Thad and Taylor. The question was, would she even want to speak up? I can tell you that I would. But Wren was easily frightened. Nervous. I wasn't convinced that she'd rat her idiot husband out.

"We won't know more until we find out some things about our guests," I said at last.

"Snooping! Yes!" Betty pumped her fist into the air.

I ignored her. "The thing we have to find out is if these people know each other more than they're letting on."

"You think they're pretending?" Lauren asked.

"It would make sense." I shrugged. "I know that no one in this room is the killer. And I know it's not Stacey or Juliette. I'm not sure about Miriam and Ned because they actually work here and were never part of the play."

Soo Jin added, "The poem is 'Eight Little Girl Scouts.' And there are…or were, eight guests."

"Now there are six," Inez added.

"And the next one drowns." Ava studied the poem. "So we basically have to keep everyone away from water."

"Which means," Betty said, "no one goes outside. Easy."

Soo Jin shook her head. "You can drown in two inches of water."

"WHAT?" The girls shouted in chorus. Apparently that never occurred to them.

The medical examiner started explaining and held the girls' rapt attention as I walked over to the murder board. I pulled a pencil out of the desk and drew a line from the lounge to the study. That was Taylor's path. It wasn't far—the enclosed front hall was the only obstacle.

Did the killer hide there after killing Taylor, or did he join everyone else in the lounge, sight unseen? The trophy had been taken from a shelf in the study, which made me think the killer had to be there when Taylor had arrived. He'd have to have been in the study previously to choose the trophy over the letter opener.

Why the trophy? It seemed meaningful somehow. The letter opener would've been an easier weapon to wield. It made more sense. Which told me that the trophy was a message. About what?

Well, the woman had been boasting of her success since arrival. Perhaps it was a metaphor for her boasting? That might be something. Who would want to kill her over that? Thad was cut from the same cloth. I couldn't see him using a trophy for that reason.

Argh! This was frustrating.

But if Taylor was killed for a particular reason, what was the point of Enos's death? He was literally killed by a fish. The man was overweight. Was that why the killer used food? As a joke?

The idea of the murders being random…just because…was terrifying. It would be way easier if there was a true motive.

There had to be more to this. These people must know each other better than they'd let on. That meant I had to interrogate each and every guest to find out. And while I was pretty sure I could find a rubber hose and some rope, common sense told me I'd have to do this very carefully.

And then, there were Ned and Miriam. Those two had the opportunity to poison Enos's fish and weren't with the rest of us when Taylor was murdered. It would've been easy enough to kill Taylor. And they'd know all about the trophy since they worked here. But why kill them? That was what tripped me up. They worked in this house before the event and didn't seem to know anyone here. The only reason they could have to go on a killing spree would be if they did it just for fun. I shuddered at the thought.

My mind rolled back to my interviews in the moments before Taylor was killed. Caroline Regent was acting strangely. And then there was that chilling comment at dinner—about death being a natural thing. But then, she was an odd one. That didn't make her a killer.

Sitting at the desk, I pulled out a notepad and listed the guests. I needed to find out if there was a unique reason—beyond it being a fundraiser—why each one of them came to this event. Right off the bat, Enos and Dennis seemed out of place here. Not many single young men would come to a Girl Scout mystery night.

It made sense that the Kasinskis were here. They loved children and had given a great deal of money to the Girl Scouts over the years. And Taylor was a former Scout. I could see her being here to relive her glory days.

And Thad and Wren? Did Thad want to come because of Taylor? Or had Wren signed up so they could do something together? The couple didn't seem to get along. Thad barely noticed his wife even existed. Or was there a darker motive—

could Wren have signed them up and then put on this scatterbrained act in order to catch Taylor and Thad together?

That left Caroline. Why was she here? She didn't like people. She admitted that. So why come alone to an event where the socially inept woman would have to mingle? Did she have a score to settle with Taylor? She had been CEO of an insurance company, and Caroline was a doctor. They could've crossed swords, so to speak.

"HELP! PLEASE! HELP!" Wren's voice was clear and coming from two rooms over.

I turned to the girls. "Stay here and lock the door behind you. Don't let anyone in but me. Got it?"

I took off in the direction of the scream. Soo Jin was right behind me. I heard the bolt thrown behind us and the sound of a chair wedging under the door. Smart girls.

Not again, I thought as I ran past Dennis's room toward Thad and Wren's room. The others were crowding the doorway. Why hadn't they gone inside to help? We pushed through and entered the room.

This was new.

Thad was face down in a bowl of some sort of gelatin substance. The hair on the back of his head was dark. Wet.

"Did you touch him or anything around him?" Soo Jin asked his wife as she kneeled to take his pulse. She shook her head at me. Thad was dead.

CHAPTER SEVEN

"Everybody back to your rooms!" I shouted at everyone who'd gathered in the hallway after hearing Wren's call for help. They cleared the area immediately.

Wren stood over her husband's body. "I didn't touch him. I ran down to the kitchen for a sealed bottle of water. Thad said he wouldn't drink anything else here anymore in case it was poisoned."

"You went alone?" I asked.

The woman nodded before sitting on the edge of the bed. I looked around the room but didn't see any water bottle. Was she lying, or had she tucked it away? It was strange that nervous little Wren would run off alone with a killer on the loose.

Thad was on the floor, his face submerged in a clear, gooey substance. From the look of the back of his head, it seemed he'd been bludgeoned. So why the bowl?

"Tell me what happened when you returned," I said, trying to distract the woman from Soo Jin's examination.

"Oh." She turned her gaze to me. "I knocked on the door, but he didn't answer. Then I tried the doorknob and found out he hadn't locked it behind me. This is what I found when I came in." She looked at the body. "Is he dead?"

I sat down next to her. "Yes. I'm so sorry."

There were no tears. No trembling. The fragile, nervous act was completely gone. The woman next to me was calm and emotionless. Was she in shock?

Dr. Regent came into the room. "I heard screaming. I was in the bathroom. What's going on?"

She took one look at the body and Soo Jin and gave Wren a once-over. Then she pulled an afghan from the foot of the bed and wrapped the woman before leaving the room.

"She thinks she might be in shock," Soo Jin said.

Sure enough, the doctor returned with a bottle of brandy that she said she got from downstairs and asked Wren to drink from it, which she did.

I'm not a doctor. I got that as Thad's wife she might be in shock. But I found Wren's behavior strange. The woman had been a jittery mess since she'd arrived. Now that her husband was dead, she'd become kind of normal. Did she kill Thad and Taylor? It would fit. The perfect motive. And where was the water bottle? Should I ask her now or save it for an interrogation later? For the thousandth time since lunch, I wished that Rex were here.

"Dr. Regent," Soo Jin said, "could you take Wren to your room?"

Caroline nodded and whisked the new widow away.

"Do you think that's a good idea?" I asked as I knelt beside her. "Either woman could be the killer."

Soo Jin looked at me. "Not a clue. But it will give me a chance to examine her late husband without upsetting her—and that seems like the priority now. Examining the crime scene before she can change things is critical. Help me turn him over."

We rolled him onto his right shoulder then onto his back. Thad's eyes were closed, and his face was completely covered with whatever this was. I touched it and rubbed it between my fingers.

"I'm probably way off," I said. "But this feels like personal lubricant."

The medical examiner nodded. "I think it is too. Glycerin based."

"What's a huge bowl filled with lube doing in here?" I asked as I started to search the room.

Under the bed I found six bottles of lubricant—all empty. Using a coat hanger to drag them out, I showed them to Soo Jin. The poem popped into my mind.

"Did he drown in it?"

Soo Jin shrugged. "I'm not sure. The killer struck him on the back of the head first, I think. Then when he was unconscious, pushed his face into this bowl." She opened his mouth and peered inside.

"It looks like he swallowed some. It's possible." Soo Jin looked at me. "But it would be more like suffocation than drowning."

"Yes, but drowning is in the poem. The blow on the head was to render him unconscious in order to drown him. I just don't understand why he'd use this stuff."

You know that moment when you inappropriately get the giggles? Like at the funeral for a Somali pirate or a 90th jubilee for a saintly nun in Peru? The sensation started in my throat and rose up until I was in hysterics.

"You're not helping," Soo Jin said.

"He drowned in lube!" I kept my voice down. "You don't think that's funny?"

She sighed. "Yes. It's funny. But I have to be professional about this."

That kind of took the wind out of my sails a bit. I thought maybe I was losing my mind.

"Tell me about the head wound," I said.

"I won't know until I shave his head. And examine his lungs to see if he drowned. But I'd say it was something blunt. Like a baseball bat, maybe."

"Well, I guess we know for sure that these murders were premeditated. Someone brought in cyanide to kill Enos and six bottles of lubricant to kill Thad. I think it's safe to say it's one killer."

Soo Jin stood up and looked at the body. "I wish it weren't true, but I think you're right."

"I wonder what the killer thought when they found out you were here."

"What's that?" she asked.

"The killer didn't realize there'd be a medical examiner on site."

Soo Jin shook her head. "I don't think that makes any difference. These crimes are pretty obvious. There are other ways to drown someone. And poison someone without it looking like poison."

"I have to think they aren't happy you're here. We're storing the bodies in the basement and collecting evidence in bags. The killer might have thought that the guests here would trample all over the scene and they'd get away with it."

"I don't know that the evidence is safe," she said. "We've been storing it in the basement. Everyone probably knows that."

"The killer will be more careful now. He knows the list of suspects is shrinking and that we are investigating."

We took an extra sheet from the closet and wrapped Thad's body in it, trying to decide if it was worth navigating two sets of stairs with the corpse. The possibility of leaving it in the room was tempting. But then, where would Wren stay?

A loud thunderclap indicated that the storm hadn't let up.

I knocked on Dennis's door, but he told us to go away. When I said we needed his help with Thad, he didn't answer.

"Thad needs to go to the basement, but because of the girls, I think we should leave him here for the time being." Soo Jin wiped her face with her forearm.

I agreed. Carrying another man, this time down two flights of stairs, was daunting. Instead, we collected up the evidence and bagged it, taking it to our room.

The girls had created a fortress. And they weren't letting anyone in.

"Come on!" I insisted. "It's Merry and Dr. Body!"

Betty's voice drifted through the door. "What's the password?"

Password? We didn't set up a password. But it was a good idea for the future.

"Girls," Soo Jin said, "please let us in."

"Password?" Betty said again.

For a moment I thought about busting in the door. But that would remove one of our main defenses.

"I guess we're going to have to figure out what the password is," I mumbled to Soo Jin. "And then I'll kill them."

She suppressed a smile.

"Can you give us a hint?" I asked the door.

There was some mumbling before Betty announced, "Who was the breaststroke swimmer from Norway in the 1964 Olympics?"

"You're joking," I replied. "How could we know that?"

"If you don't say the password," Betty said, "how do we know it's really you?"

"How can we tell you the password if you made it up after we left?"

There was dead silence on the other side as I imagined four little girls staring at each other. The bolt was thrown, and the doorknob turned.

Once inside with the door locked behind us, I said, "While I like the idea of a password, I think that all of us should be aware of it…before we leave the room." And then I stopped dead in my tracks.

Betty had something red smeared all over her neck, and Inez was holding a four-foot-long stuffed Marlin with similar red marks on its pointy nose. Where had she gotten that? In the corner, Ava was face down on a dinner plate.

"Are you guys reenacting the murders?" Soo Jin asked.

"Yes," Ava shouted, her face still on the plate.

Betty turned around, and Inez stabbed her in the neck with the giant game fish. Betty fell to the floor and started to twitch violently as foam came out of her mouth.

"Toothpaste?" Soo Jin asked.

I nodded. "You have to admit—they're creative."

This wasn't a bad idea, and I appreciated the effort. It still only told us what we already knew. That doesn't mean I stopped Inez from stabbing Betty over and over. You have to take your entertainment where you can get it when locked in a big house with three dead bodies and a killer.

Lauren looked into the bowl I was carrying. "What's that?"

The other girls stopped what they were doing and crowded around. I had no idea what to say.

"Glycerine!" Betty said. "Are we making bombs?"

"What's up with you and bombs?" I asked, remembering the shape charges sitting at the bottom of the lake.

"It's not for bombs," Soo Jin said. "But you're right. It's…um…a glycerin-based substance."

"What's it used for?" Ava stuck her finger in it, and I pulled the bowl away.

Soo Jin and I exchanged glances. She probably was silently suggesting that we give them a very technical medical excuse, while I was trying to tell her through telepathy that I wasn't going to tell them anything.

I tried something else. "Thad Gable is dead."

That got their attention. Inez ran to the murder board and took up one of the little Post-it figures.

"Where does he go?" she asked.

"In his room," I answered. "Two doors over."

Betty was prepared for this. They'd made the facsimile of the board for the second floor while we were gone, in addition to acting out the crimes. I didn't think we were gone that long.

The little figure went into Thad and Wren's room as Inez uncapped a pen. "How did he die?"

"Struck on the back of the head then drowned in this." I indicated the bowl.

Inez thought about it for a moment before drawing a dent in the figure's head and little waves of water going up his nose. The attention to detail was impressive. Meanwhile, Ava was sculpting Thad face down in a bowl. I only knew who it was by the bowl, because Thad's figure looked like a penguin with two heads. These girls were seriously in need of some art instruction.

Lauren folded her arms over her chest. "You're going to have to tell us everything."

She had a point. Soo Jin and I explained what we'd seen when we entered the room. They listened carefully, even as I described Wren's strange behavior.

"Dr. Regent showed up late?" Betty asked. "And she was walking around alone?"

I nodded.

"She did it," the girl said. "She's our killer. Only the killer would wander around alone."

I shook my head. "I don't know if that's true. If she thought everyone was in their rooms, she'd have felt safe."

"But she didn't know Thad was dead," Lauren said.

Betty nodded. "She did if she was the killer."

That's when I noticed the large pad of paper and easel in the corner.

"How did that get in here?" I asked as I scanned each face. And that was when I noticed Betty's hair and Lauren's hair were wet.

"Did you go out the window?" I gasped.

"We had to get some more materials," Lauren said. "You'd notice us in the hallway. So we went out this window, climbed down the drainpipe, and went in through the conservatory."

Betty picked it up. "We found this in a closet in the study and ran it upstairs."

What? I couldn't believe it! I was angry and stunned, trying to decide how to handle this, when Soo Jin stepped in.

"That was a terrible idea," she said gently. "You could've fallen or been killed."

The girls actually hung their heads. They loved the doctor, and I guess her being upset made them sad. I had to admit, it calmed me down a little.

"Wait," I said. "The conservatory window was open? Earlier we'd checked all the windows. They were all locked on the inside."

Lauren shook her head. "No, it wasn't. We taped over the bolt on one of the windows, just in case."

Betty added, "You would've thought you'd locked it, but you didn't. Turning the bolt wouldn't have released it because of the tape."

Well, at least we had a place to write ideas.

Since my handwriting was terrible, Soo Jin was selected to make a list of the guests and who the victims were so far.

There was a knock on the door. It was Stacey. Oh, right! I'd forgotten we were going to take a shift in the hallway. I opened the door and stepped out into the hallway so she wouldn't see what the girls had been up to.

She looked around nervously. "Are you ready?"

"I should check in on Wren," I said.

"She just went back to her room to get a bottle of water. Caroline walked her there, and both went back to Dr. Regent's room. I just saw them."

So there was a bottle of water. I must've missed it.

"I'll relieve you in a few hours," Soo Jin said as she made notes.

Stacey had dragged two chairs just outside our room. It was quiet in the hall. The railing that surrounded the staircase was the only thing obstructing our view of the entire floor, and that was only three feet high.

We could see the door to every room. Either the killer was in their room, planning to kill Thad, or they got lucky when Thad sent Wren downstairs for a bottle of water. Did the killer know that would happen?

"I can't believe this," the Girl Scout employee said sadly. "If you'd told me one person would die at our fundraiser, I wouldn't have believed it."

I patted her hand. "None of this is your fault."

She gave me a look I couldn't interpret. "JD thinks it's yours."

JD? Juliette Dowd? Was that what her co-workers called her? Of course she'd think it was me. She hated me. If I went to prison, that would get me out of the way so she could pursue Rex. It probably didn't matter to her that Rex had no interest. But was she the killer here? I didn't think so.

"Yeah, well, Juliette doesn't like me."

Stacey laughed. "You can say that again."

"It's pretty obvious, isn't it?"

"She says she was contracted to marry Rex," Stacey added. "Is that true?"

I sighed. "When they were little kids, their parents verbally discussed the two of them getting married. It was never legally binding, and Rex had no interest in dating or marrying her. It's kind of sad, really."

We were speaking very quietly, but since we were outside of Enos's room, I figured no one was listening. Our job was simple. To sit here and make sure no one left their room. Since each room had a bathroom, there was no reason to go anywhere.

The thrum of rain on the roof was making me sleepy. Carrying bodies down to the basement, running around chasing a killer, and worrying about everyone was exhausting, to say the least.

"If only we'd done this an hour earlier," Stacey said. "Thad Gable would be alive."

Wren said she went downstairs to get a bottle of water. I racked my brain but didn't remember seeing a bottle of water anywhere in the room. And yet Stacey just saw Wren go to her room to retrieve the bottle, so maybe Wren wasn't lying. Or, she already had a bottle. Wren could've killed Thad without even leaving the room. That was a possibility. I'd kill Thad if I was married to him.

Did that mean Wren was the killer? She certainly had a motive to kill Taylor. This would've worked out well for taking her husband and his lover out at the same time. The whole flighty thing could be an act. People weren't always what they seemed.

The only problem with Wren as the killer was Enos. Why kill him? Practice for taking out the others? As a red herring to throw us off the track? That idea had merit because it would mean no one else would die. Wren could very well be Kevin. And the great thing about that was I knew I could take her.

I wanted to talk about this theory, but should I discuss this with Stacey? How much did she want to know? She'd stayed in the background during this whole thing, which was probably for the best.

"I don't know if it would've made a difference," I said finally. The less she knew, the better.

"Well." She looked around the corridor. "It really would've been a fun event."

"I have a question you might be able to answer." I realized she had info I could use. "How did you get these attendees? Did you send out a bunch of invites and limit it to eight? Did you only ask these folks?"

For a moment I was afraid she wouldn't answer—like there was some sort of Girl Scout special event secrecy rule or something. But the blonde relaxed a little, seemingly happy to discuss something other than murder.

"We only have about a dozen donors who give at that level annually. Audrey Deivers came up with the idea initially and volunteered her house. We sent out invitations, and these eight accepted."

"What about the other four?" I asked. "The ones who didn't accept?"

"Two couples—they were going to Greece on a cruise together. They left a week ago."

I thought of something else. "Did everyone who accepted know who was attending?"

She shook her head. "I don't think so. Word might have gotten around. But I doubt it. I don't think Wren would've come if she knew Taylor was going to be here."

So the guests most likely didn't know who was going to be here. Which brought us back to the random killer theory. I didn't like that one.

"Did anyone know my troop was going to be here?" That would explain the last part of the poem about the CIA.

Stacey narrowed her eyes and cocked her head to the right. "I don't think so. You weren't on the invitation."

"And what about Miriam and Ned—did anyone know about them?"

She shook her head.

The staff had been at the back of my mind during this whole thing, but I was still on the fence about their involvement. Mostly they kept to themselves and stayed in their cabin. They were the only people who actually belonged here, and it was unlikely that they moved in the same social circles as the guests.

However, if it was Miriam and Ned and they were just killing us off for fun, it would make sense since they had access to the fish that poisoned Enos, knew about the trophy that killed Taylor, and knew their way around the house. I thought about seeing that shadow in the lounge when the first sculpture was broken. Whoever it was hadn't come out of the doorway or I would've seen them. The problem was, where did they go?

There was probably another broken sculpture now. I wanted to check, but I couldn't leave Stacey alone up here, and if we both left, the killer might strike again.

I followed another train of thought. "Do *you* know these people well?"

"Not really. I'm mostly in charge of the camps, so I'm not involved too much with administration. The CEO and VP of Finance probably knows them better. I've seen a few of them at parties we've thrown whenever we update one of the camps. I've talked to almost all of them a bit."

"What can you tell me about the Gables?" I asked.

"Well, Thad is a famous attorney, and Wren is involved in the art world. They haven't been married very long. I think a couple of years, maybe?"

"I didn't know that. I'd have thought they'd been together longer."

She shook her head. "In fact, Thad brought Taylor to a fundraiser a month or so before his wedding. We thought it was odd, but then they're both donors and had been invited. So maybe it wasn't so weird."

That was interesting. "I know this sounds like gossip, but it might really help. Do you think they were having an affair?"

She looked uncomfortable with the question. "I'm sorry. I really couldn't say."

Moving on. "What about the Kasinskis?"

Stacey smiled. "I do know them. Married fifty years. Always lived here. Violet was a Girl Scout back in the day. Very generous donors and the nicest people. As much as they love kids, it's sad they couldn't have any."

"Why's that, do you think?" I tried to sound casual.

She shrugged. "No idea. They never discussed it. But rumor has it that they tried for decades before giving up."

"I wonder why they didn't adopt."

"Violet once told me that they channeled their energy instead into helping children's causes. That's why they are so great for the Council. I honestly can't say anything bad about them." She frowned. "Which makes me worry. You don't think the killer will target them too?"

I thought about this. "From the poem, it looks like almost all of them will be targeted, because one of them is the killer."

"And you," Stacey said. "The last line is about you, right?"

I nodded. "I think so." I had an idea. "I think I should search Enos's room."

Stacey's eyes flew open wide. "But what about watching things here?"

"You stand in the doorway, in sight of me and the hall. Call out if you see anyone, and I'll be there to handle it."

It took a few seconds before she agreed. I mean, we were sitting right outside Enos's room. It was a perfect opportunity. In fact, I don't know why we hadn't thought of it sooner. Enos's things should still be inside. Maybe I could find a clue. And the best part was—it would keep me awake. My energy was dangerously low.

We propped open the door with one of the chairs. Stacey stood in the doorway, her back against the frame so she could see both the hall and inside the room.

Enos's room was pretty small. One lone twin bed and one dresser. It had a tiny bathroom with a stool, sink, and shower stall. Two windows were being hammered with rain. A suitcase sat on the floor. I checked the closet, but it was empty.

Lifting the suitcase to the bed, I carefully opened it. I don't like opening things if I don't know what's in them. It all dates back to those little music boxes you wind up until the clown pops out.

It wasn't a toy that made me jumpy around them. It was a case I had in Uzbekistan. My contact there hid a thumb drive inside of a toy for me to retrieve. Unfortunately, the Russians knew about it and hid something of their own…a pop gun that shot a ricin bullet. It narrowly missed me.

Ricin is a nasty way to go and a Russian trademark. Riley pulled us out of there after that happened, and shortly after we were stationed in the much safer drug lord countryside of Colombia.

Nothing popped out of Enos's suitcase. In fact, it was almost empty. The man only had extra underwear and socks inside—which meant he planned to wear his outfit the entire weekend.

After a quick glance to make sure Stacey was all good, I started working my way through the pockets. I found a Dopp kit with the usual toiletries and another pair of shoes. And in a hidden panel, I found five dozen Twinkies. I'm not kidding. I counted. I even toyed with eating one or two for the sugar rush but decided against it. In fact, I was starting to think I was just a dozen shy of becoming Enos. Maybe I should eat more salad. Can you put Pizza Rolls in salad?

"Anything?" Stacey whispered.

I shook my head and closed the suitcase. Next I tried the dresser. All of the drawers were empty. I took each one out and examined it, including the underside. Nothing. Using my cell as a flashlight, I checked under the bed and dresser, where I found a case of candy bars but nothing that even resembled a clue. I did put a couple of bars in my pocket for later. I'm not an idiot.

"There's nothing there." I sighed as I pulled my chair out into the hall and closed the door.

What did I really expect to find? The man was the first victim. He obviously wasn't the killer. If there'd just been some connection to Thad or Taylor, I could've had an idea who the murderer was.

Instead, I had connections between Thad and Taylor. And without the water bottle, Wren was starting to look guilty. But first, I needed more information about the other guests.

"What do you know about Enos and Dennis?" I asked Stacey once we were seated again.

"Dennis didn't want to come," Stacey whispered. "His parents haven't been very happy with him just lying around their house for years. They were originally going to join us, but then his father got called out of the country for work, and they insisted that Dennis take their place since they'd already paid."

"Was that unusual—for Dennis's parents to miss the event?"

Stacey cocked her head to the side, thinking. "You know what? Now that you say it, they often miss events. They buy the tickets at the drop of a hat, but later they always find some sort of conflict in their schedule." She shrugged. "I guess they just aren't very organized."

That was interesting. "What else do you know about Dennis?"

She shook her head. "Nothing."

"And Enos?"

There was a bit of hesitation. "That's another matter. Enos is…was fairly new to us. From what I understood, he gave money away just to avoid taxes. There was talk that he was bored with life and always looking for something interesting. Frankly, we were shocked when he accepted."

The door to my room opened, and Soo Jin appeared. "The girls want to go to the library to find books to read. Is that okay?"

I nodded. And watched Soo Jin herd them out of the room and downstairs. Poor kids. They were wide awake with all the excitement and probably bored out of their skulls. Then I remembered the sculptures, so I called out to Soo Jin to look in the lounge.

A moment later, she called up from the bottom of the stairs. "Another one of the…things…I think it's a cow…"

I heard Lauren yell, "Badger."

Soo Jin corrected, "The badger is broken."

She promised to hurry. I looked around. Enos's room was behind me, with our room on my right. Dennis was between our room and the Gables'. Taylor's room was next to theirs, with Stacey and Juliette's room in the corner. Caroline's room was next, with the Kasinskis in the corner on my left. From eight rooms, only six were occupied now. How many more would become empty in the next few hours?

The storm had to let up soon. Tomorrow we'd find a way to signal the shore and get the boat back here with the authorities. That was my mission. To get the rest of these folks off the island alive. If only I had a gun.

Soo Jin and the girls came up the stairs and went back into the room, their little arms full of books. Each girl gave us a little nod as she passed.

I relaxed a little.

"What about Taylor?" I asked.

Stacey rolled her eyes, which surprised me because I'd never seen her be anything other than professional. Taylor was obviously a source of irritation. It was like watching a dam break.

"She's been involved with us for years. Never as a volunteer, but as a donor. As she climbed the corporate ladder, her donations grew, but she drove us insane, constantly criticizing everything we did. She was on the board of directors for two years. Drove them crazy. We lost three great volunteers while she was on. No one was sad when she resigned."

Did *anyone* like Taylor? Besides Thad, that is?

"How about Dr. Regent? Tell me about her."

Stacey tapped her chin. "Well, she and Taylor were friends for years. Met at Girl Scout Camp as kids."

What? I never would've guessed that! The two women didn't so much as look at each other this whole time. I guess that should've been a giveaway. In the spy world, you can often tell if people are connected by how they ignore each other. How had I missed it?

"Are you sure? They hadn't said two words to each other all day?" Of course, this was partly due to the fact that Taylor was now dead.

"I'm sure." Stacey nodded. "Taylor brought Caroline to a couple of fundraisers her first year with us. They both told me they'd grown up together. I have no idea what happened to split them up, but they were fast friends originally."

This was interesting news. And it moved Caroline up to the top of the suspect list. A doctor could easily get ahold of cyanide and would know just how much it would take to kill a guy as big as Enos. If she and Taylor had a bad breakup, it would explain the violent way Taylor was murdered. And a doctor would know exactly where the jugular vein was. She would know where to hit Thad on the head so he'd be out cold and easy to drown.

The hair stood up on my arms. Caroline was the only one to see Taylor leave the room. And she came late to see Thad's body. She also had no problem running downstairs alone for brandy—especially if it was because she felt safe since she was the killer.

Could it really be this easy?

Hmmm…but what about motive? I understood her killing Taylor. And maybe the reason she'd stopped hanging with Caroline was because she'd been having an affair with Thad. But once more Enos's murder didn't seem to fit.

"What is it?" Stacey studied my expression.

"I think we need to search Taylor's room too," I said.

And then find a way to catch the killer before they killed again.

CHAPTER EIGHT

We moved quietly around the railing to Taylor's room and took up the same positions we had for our search of Enos's room. The bedroom was exactly the same, except that Taylor had filled her dresser and closet with clothes. As I went through it all, a little voice in the back of my brain insisted I was missing something.

I started back at the beginning and went through the room, slowly searching under and behind furniture, inside clothes pockets and bags in hopes of finding whatever it was. After a good twenty minutes, my search yielded nothing. A yawn broke out, and I realized I'd been up for a long time. My overactive imagination was most likely due to a lack of sleep.

Finally, Stacey and I retreated back to our seats near my room. The hall was quiet, but then again, it was getting late, so most people were probably sleeping. Still, I wasn't going anywhere. Just because everyone else was locked up, it didn't mean I shouldn't keep an eye open.

I used to be pretty good at stakeouts. And I could stay up all night if I had to—usually due to enough sugar to give an elephant the jitters. This sugar was loosely disguised as food. Something like cake or candy or in China once—chocolate-covered beetles. I washed those down with an energy drink, and if you had plugged me into a socket, I could have powered a small village for days.

The candy bars I'd swiped from Enos's room were calling to me. The problem with a sugar buzz that would kill a grown man was that eventually you came down and slid into a coma that lasted at least two days. I didn't have any time for that. I would need to stay up the old-fashioned way—talking.

"Stacey," I said. "What about Juliette?" There was a spike of adrenaline when I said her name out loud. Perfect!

The woman looked confused. "What do you mean?"

"What's she like?" I decided to go with.

Stacey took a deep breath. "She's okay. A bit gung ho and a smidge too obsessed with rules, but she loves her job and loves Girl Scouts."

"Does she get along with others?" I asked. "Other than me, I mean?"

She frowned for a moment. "Yes. I mean, if you don't do everything according to the book, she can freak out. But you'd have a hard time finding a better cheerleader for girls."

Did the Council not know how this woman had plagued me? And if not, was it even worth bringing up here? We did have bigger problems to deal with. Maybe I should bury the hatchet and act like nothing was wrong. After all, Juliette hadn't sniped at me once since I arrived.

"Oh!" The blonde's eyes grew wide. "You mean the fact that she hates you!"

I stood corrected. "Yes. Am I the only one?"

She shook her head. "No. Juliette hates you, and the Boy Scouts."

"Great," I mumbled.

"You certainly don't think she's the killer, do you? I can't even imagine that."

I shook my head. "No. I don't think either one of you is the killer."

"I can't stop wondering about Ned and Miriam," Stacey said.

"Do you guys know them?" Now, here was something I hadn't thought of.

She thought for a moment. "Not really. I know they work for the Deivers family and have for at least a few years."

"Would they know the other guests here?"

She shrugged. "I don't think it's likely. Mrs. Deivers must trust them though."

Could Audrey Deivers be involved? I pictured the blonde as a puppet master—manipulating her staff into killing these people. Maybe she never left the island and was here somewhere.

A skittering sound came from my right. "Did you hear that?"

Stacey looked pale as she nodded.

It sounded like a kind of clattering sound on the floor. Was the killer afoot?

"Gertrude!" Stacey squealed as she bent and scooped the bunny up. "You scared us! Naughty bunny!"

The rabbit was larger than I thought. Maybe the size of my cat, Martini. She had white fur, huge eyes, and two long ears that hung down. Her pink nose twitched as she tried to figure out what was going on.

I reached over and scratched between her eyes. She was the softest thing I'd ever touched.

"Should we hold on to her?" Stacey asked. "To keep her safe?"

My girls were never going to forgive my answer. "No. She'll be safer hiding in the walls."

Stacey set the bunny on the floor, and she scrambled away adorably. At least there was one person (well, besides the girls or Soo Jin) in this house I didn't have to worry about. We spent the next hour or so lost in our own thoughts.

I was no closer to finding the killer, which frustrated me. On the one hand, who could solve three murders in half a day? Rex certainly never had, and he was trained for it. But then again, we were isolated, and whoever was killing us off appeared to know their way around the house.

The list of suspects was dwindling, however. Dennis, Wren, Caroline, and the Kasinskis, with Miriam and Ned in a weird second sort of place, with Audrey Deivers as an alternate.

It was strange how I was torn on the issue of Ned and Miriam. Neither servant was in the room when Enos died, but had access to his lunch. And they were the only ones not with us when Taylor was murdered in the study. Could they have killed Thad? Did they see Wren downstairs and think that this was their chance? The rest of us were in our rooms.

And what did we really know about them, except for the fact that they worked here and lived in a cottage out back? They certainly knew the grounds well enough and could probably move around unnoticed.

Looks like those two were now higher up on the list. Alright, so let's work backwards. Who was at the bottom? That was easy—Dennis, Arthur, and Violet. Dennis seemed too lazy to kill people. And I was pretty sure Violet was too weak to have struck both Taylor and Thad down.

But what about Arthur? The man was about my height. He had some girth around his middle, and his amiable personality could be all a lie. But then, he didn't have the connections to any of the deceased, and Violet had been by his side the entire time.

Wren and Caroline were at the top of my list. Wren had definite motive and opportunity. If she knew about Taylor and Thad's alleged affair, she'd have every reason to kill them both. And Wren was the last person to see her husband alive and the first to see him dead. She could easily have lied to us about what happened.

Caroline had a past with Taylor. They'd been close since childhood. Did Caroline hold a grudge when whatever broke them up happened? Was Thad the reason the two friends split up? If so, she'd have motive to kill both. And she was the only one who saw Taylor leave the lounge for the study. Which meant she could have slipped away and killed Taylor, coming back before anyone noticed she was gone. We were all distracted by the bunny. Who knew what really happened?

Caroline's bedroom was three over from Thad's. It wouldn't have been hard to slip across the hallway if she saw Wren go downstairs. And, as a doctor, she knew the right place to strike someone to render them out with one blow. Not to mention that she'd know exactly where in the throat to stab Taylor with one shot.

And then there were the methods of murder. Taylor was speared by a gold trophy. Both Wren and Caroline could have used something like that to make a statement. Taylor always seemed to think she was the best at everything. The trophy could've been a sarcastic metaphor.

As for the bowl of lubricant—if Thad was having an affair with Taylor, Wren would be more likely to choose that method of murder to make a statement of sorts. But if Taylor dropped Caroline for Thad, it was possible she could use the same thing. To be honest, the lube gag was pretty tough to explain to the girls. Maybe I should've gone with the pipe bomb idea. Vaseline was sometimes used when putting a pipe bomb together. But if I had gone with that explanation, for months I'd have parents asking why their daughters were so interested in K-Y Jelly. The thought made me a little nauseous.

My mind was starting to wander. I needed to get back on focus. And that meant my new top suspects—Wren and Caroline. The only problem with Wren or Caroline being the killer—was Enos. Neither woman seemed to have any connection to the man.

Somehow I needed to talk to both women. And both women were currently holed up in Caroline's room. Whoa. Were they in it together?

The scenarios came together in my head like a jigsaw puzzle. It would make sense. Both women working together to get the people who'd betrayed them out of the way! How did I not see it before?

Wren and Caroline working together would explain everything! Caroline slipping away unseen to kill Taylor while Wren kept watch, and Wren killing Thad with Caroline's advice or even help! They could be celebrating right now! As for Enos—I liked the idea of him being a red herring to throw us off the next two victims. It was kind of brilliant. They must've thought that the death of Enos would put Taylor and Thad off a little, but not too much. They needed Taylor to slip away, thinking she was meeting Thad. She couldn't be paralyzed with fear to do that.

Very carefully, I tiptoed past Arthur and Violet's room to Caroline's and pressed my ear against the door. I couldn't hear anything. It would've been so nice to hear them plotting or celebrating. Or better yet—confessing to the crime out loud for no apparent reason.

Stacey gave me a questioning look as I walked back to her. I whispered that I was working on an idea and went back to my seat and my thoughts.

If Caroline and Wren were the killers, did that mean the murders would end? Or would they think that I'd thought of this, so they'd kill one or two more people in order to confuse things even more? Sadly, because of the poem, it didn't seem likely. If the poem was right, more people were going to die.

I didn't want anything to happen to the Kasinskis or to Dennis. But they might not be the only ones in danger. It was always possible that the killers would attack everyone on my safe list, just to make things more confusing.

Soo Jin opened the door and stepped out. Across the hall, a sleepy Juliette opened her door and joined us. The weight of the day started taking its toll on me the minute they arrived. Stacey went straight to her room, and I heard the door lock with a *snick.*

Part of me wanted to send Juliette away. But I was drooping. I needed sleep. No, there'd be time for me to tell Soo Jin my theories in the morning. Giving her a nod, I went into the room. All four girls were sound asleep, with the lights on. I locked the door behind me and fell onto my bed, fully clothed. My last thought was wondering if I could attach a digital recorder to Gertrude so I could listen as she ran through the walls…

CHAPTER NINE

A huge boom of thunder woke me with a start, and I saw the four girls up, beds made, reading books.

"What time is it?" I yawned.

"Eight in the morning," Betty said, her voice dripping with disapproval.

I struggled to sit up and stared at the black clouds outside the window. "It's still storming? How is that possible?"

The girls nodded. "Dr. Body is brushing her teeth."

"Too bad she's not using the app," Lauren added. "We've come up with some more modifications, and it would be helpful to observe the app in use." She looked at me hopefully.

I shook my head, "No way. I'm not going to be stabbed or shocked just for brushing my teeth."

Inez rolled her eyes. "We haven't weaponized it. Yet."

"There's a lot of testing we have to do," Ava agreed. "And focus groups. We need to do focus groups."

"What are those?" Betty asked.

Ava never liked to seem like she didn't know what she was talking about. "You get a bunch of people together." The wheels turned behind her eyes as she searched for an answer. "From Iceland. And you put them in a room and release a fly to see who can focus on it." The girl folded her arms over her chest smugly.

"What does that have to do with the app?" Lauren pressed.

Ava glared at them. "It's part of the process. Everyone knows that."

Ava's idea was certainly better than the truth. It would be even more epic if you gave everyone a gun with laser sights and money to the first person who shot the fly. Again—nothing that related to a toothbrushing app, but it would be fun.

Seconds later, a refreshed and not-tired-at-all Soo Jin emerged from the bathroom, looking like she'd had eight hours of sleep, no stress, and a shower, and had definitely not been electrocuted by her phone when brushing her teeth.

It took me ten minutes to take a quick shower and get dressed. I joined the girls as they were lined up by the door.

"Breakfast," Inez insisted. "I'm starving."

The others quickly agreed.

Soo Jin opened the door, and I joined the line. The hallway was empty, but the dining room was full. Well, not quite. There were three empty chairs. The delectable scent of bacon and eggs came from the kitchen as my stomach rumbled. The girls sat at their table, and Soo Jin and I took our seats.

Miriam entered with a platter of eggs, bacon, and toast. Ned followed with a tray of chocolate chip waffles, which he set on the kids' table. So. Not. Fair.

The only good news was that at least everyone left survived the night.

"It's still storming," Dennis said glumly.

My eyes lingered for a brief moment on Caroline and Wren, who were sitting next to each other, across from me. Were they secretly thrilled that the storm covered their tracks? The only problem they had to worry about was, how would they escape before I nailed them?

"Arthur didn't sleep very well." Violet patted him on the back. "He doesn't do well with storms, poor thing."

Her husband took her hand and kissed it. It was adorable. Once again, I hoped that Rex and I would be like that at their age. That would be nice. We weren't exactly like that now—neither of us being big on public displays of affection. We were affectionate in our own way—like when Rex cleaned up after Philby knocked everything off the counter for no reason. Or how I shared my Pizza Rolls with him…sometimes.

"At least we still have power," Caroline grunted. "No landline though. I checked."

"We always lose the phone," Ned said as he put a plate of hash browns on the table, "when there's a storm. They never did a good job installing it to begin with."

"Were you two in your cottage all night?" I asked.

Ned glared at me. "Yes, if you must know. We were."

It didn't matter what he said because he could be lying. And unless I found a polygraph test in the basement or truth serum in the medicine cabinet, I'd have no way of knowing if what he said was the truth or not.

We devoured breakfast, our eyes avoiding looking at the three empty chairs.

"I hope we can go home today." Wren shivered. "Thanks, Caroline, for putting me up last night."

The doctor nodded but said nothing.

As far as I knew, the single rooms only had one bed in them. If that was true, where did Wren sleep? Maybe there was more to their relationship than I'd thought.

"I couldn't spend the night in that room with Thad's body." Wren shuddered.

Was she acting? Maybe not. Even if she was the killer, it would be unlikely she'd want to remain in that room.

"I think we need some answers." Betty narrowed her eyes from the kiddie table.

Wren shook her head. "I don't care about answers right now. I want to go home."

Spoken like a true psycho killer.

We finished eating and as a group carried our plates to the kitchen. Miriam and Ned were nowhere to be found, so we piled them on the counter. Where were they? And why were they gone? If we spent another night here, I was going to follow them.

These old houses had secrets, but the layout was too open. Unless they were going back to their cottage every time. I thought I'd need to check that place out.

As if on autopilot, everyone made their way back to the lounge and sat in their original seats. It was depressing.

"Now what?" Dennis asked. "Are we just going to sit here until the storm quits or someone else gets killed?"

It was a fair question.

Caroline didn't even look up from her book *Infectious Diseases of Iowa*. "There might not be any more murders."

Wren nodded eagerly. "That's true!"

Aha! Were the killers letting us know that we were safe now?

Arthur frowned. "Why would the killer stop?"

"Maybe"—Wren cocked her head to one side—"the killer's rage is spent. Now in the light of day, his fury is burned out."

Caroline nodded. "I think she's right."

It sure seemed like they were telling us it was safe. I needed to get Soo Jin alone so I could fill her in on my theory. And I had an idea.

"Girls." I stood. "How about we handle kitchen duty? Like good Girl Scouts?"

To my complete surprise, they jumped to their feet and filed out the door. These girls were masters of manipulation when it came to chores. When we camped, Kelly made chore charts that rivaled the organization skills of any A-type obsessive compulsive. And those girls managed to disappear every time their names were up.

I once found the four Kaitlyns hiding in a tree one hundred and fifty yards from our campsite when they were supposed to be washing dishes. When I asked what they were doing there, they answered that they were watching for forest fires. It was a shock when they spotted one. But I still made them finish their chores.

Stacey and Juliette started to rise, but I waved them off. Fortunately, Soo Jin got the hint and followed us. Once inside the room, I stationed Betty and Lauren in the doorway with dish towels. Miriam was still gone, and the dirty dishes were piled up. I needed lookouts. They knew what to do without being asked.

Inez grabbed a bottle of spray cleaner and some paper towels and started wiping off the counters, while Ava began putting food in the fridge. I guessed that they only wanted to do dishes if they thought it would help catch a killer.

I turned on the water and as I started washing dishes, quietly told Soo Jin what I'd been thinking about Caroline and Wren. The girls were listening but said nothing. Soo Jin handed

Betty and Lauren the wet dishes, and they dried them, glancing furtively into the hall.

"The idea makes a lot of sense," Soo Jin said when I was finished. "Poor Enos. He just got in the way."

I nodded. "That's what I think. And we pretty much heard it from the horses' mouths that the killings were over."

"There are TALKING HORSES HERE?" Lauren shrieked.

"The only way a horse can talk is if it's a magical unicorn." Inez nodded. She'd run out of countertops and was now sweeping the floor.

"Or," Betty added, "if it's two guys in a horse suit."

Ava rolled her eyes. "That doesn't make any sense!"

I couldn't help it. "Which part? The unicorn or the guys in a horse costume?"

She gave me a look I'd seen many times on my troop's faces—the one that said I was an idiot. "Obviously it's the costume. Unicorns are real, duh."

Lauren nodded. "I saw it in the *National Enquirer*."

Soo Jin, as a scientist, opened her mouth to correct them. Then she closed it. Maybe she liked the idea that these girls still believed in magic.

"Hey." Inez was struggling with a tall cupboard door. "I can't get this open to put the broom back."

Ava joined her, and they gave it a good hard pull, and the door flew open, knocking the girls onto the floor. After making sure they were okay, I stepped forward to check it out.

"Who puts a light in a utility cupboard?" I said as I drew near.

Sure enough, a large light fixture was attached to the ceiling. The whole cupboard was maybe five feet, six inches in height and three yards wide. And it seemed very, very deep.

"Inez," I asked, "did you get the broom out of here?"

"No. It was leaning against the wall. I thought I'd put it back though. Why?"

I turned to look at Soo Jin and the girls. "Because this isn't just a closet." And to make my point, I stepped inside and disappeared.

CHAPTER TEN

The girls and Soo Jin crowded the doorway as I found a light switch and turned it on.

"A secret passage!" Soo Jin said.

The closet emptied into a slightly bigger area, with a staircase going downstairs. I pointed at the girls.

"You four stay here. Close the door behind us, and if anyone comes in, don't let them near this closet. Dr. Body and I will see where it leads."

The girls folded their arms over their chests and scowled.

"You can play with it later. I promise," I said, crossing my heart.

That seemed to help. Soo Jin stepped into the cupboard, and the girls closed the door behind her.

"This is so cool!" she said. "Where does it go?"

I started down the stairs. "The basement, I guess. But I don't remember seeing a staircase down there. There wasn't even a door."

"Do you think this was a stop on the Underground Railroad? I've heard there were houses like this in Iowa."

My foot hit the floor below. "No idea. Maybe."

I was in some sort of narrow corridor that ran all the way to a corner on my left and made a sharp corner turn on my right. In front of me was a wall.

"The basement has fake walls!" I knocked on it and received the hollow reply.

Soo Jin hit the floor and looked around her. "Which way?"

We decided to go left. The walls were gray cinderblock with no decoration. Every few feet or so was a light fixture on the ceiling. As we turned the corner, we were confronted with another set of stairs on our left. We shrugged at each other, and I started climbing, coming to a small, confined space much like the one we'd walked through in the kitchen. There was a small door, and I slowly turned the knob and pushed.

"It's the conservatory!" I gasped as we stepped through.

The door had been painted to blend in with the décor of the wall. On this side, unless you really scrutinized it, you'd never know it was there. I wondered why the Deivers hadn't mentioned this? Did anyone else know? Most likely, the staff knew. But what about the others?

We went back downstairs and kept walking until we ran into another set of stairs, which we climbed without comment. I again turned the knob as quietly as possible and pushed the door open just a crack. If my theory was right, eventually we'd enter a room where the others were sitting.

Nothing. I stuck my head in and found myself in the study. Soo Jin followed me out, and we realized that the door was part of an enormous portrait that swung open. Nice! We retraced our steps back downstairs. Turning right at the corner, we followed a long hallway until we turned right again.

Another set of stairs. I thought about the layout of the house and ascended much more carefully. Slight pressure on the knob let in a sliver of light, and I froze. This was the lounge. The other guests were on the other side of this door. I couldn't see anyone, and the conversations were mumbled, so I closed it very carefully, and we went back down to the basement.

"It's a secret passageway that runs the perimeter of the basement and ends up in the four corner rooms," I mused. "That's how the killer broke the squirrel in the lounge after Enos was killed!"

"You said you saw a shadow in there." Soo Jin picked up my line of reasoning. "That's how the killer got in and out."

"I can't believe it!" I whispered ecstatically. "I think we just stumbled on how Kevin the Killer got around, sight unseen."

"Yes." Soo Jin sobered up. "But we can't say anything about it until the police arrive. We don't want to tip our hand, especially if your theory is right about Wren and Caroline."

Normally I could handle one or two women. But with the elderly couple and four small children around, I'd have to be sure. Soo Jin was technically on the police force, but I didn't know if hand-to-hand combat was in her skill set. The girls, on the other hand, could take on a small platoon of armed Boy Scouts and leave them crying in the dust. But Kelly would kill me if I let them fight.

"Okay," I agreed. "We'll act like we don't know what we really do know."

"Good idea," Soo Jin said. And together we made our way back up to the kitchen.

As we stepped out, Betty and Lauren gave us the thumbs-up from the doorway. I knew we'd have to let them explore later, but this wasn't the right time.

Back in the lounge, we were surprised to see only Dennis there.

"Where is everyone?" I asked. "Why didn't they stay together?"

Dennis shrugged. "Dr. Regent announced that she thinks we are all safe now and could do, you know, whatever."

Soo Jin and I looked at each other. Either Caroline really was showing her hand, or she said that because she's sick of being pent up in a roomful of people. As an introvert, that was probably her worst nightmare.

"So where are the others?" I asked.

Dennis yawned. "The old people said they were going to look for books in the library. Those two Girl Scout chicks were going to play pool, and I don't know where Wren and Dr. Regent are."

"What do you think?" I asked Soo Jin.

"Let's check out the other rooms," she said.

The girls agreed with a bit more enthusiasm than I was comfortable with, but as long as we were together, they'd be safe. After a quick check revealed that the foyer and study were empty, we found the Kasinskis were in the library, curled up in overstuffed wingback chairs, reading.

"Hello, ladies!" Arthur waved and went back to his book.

"Are you guys alright?" I asked.

Violet nodded. "Oh yes! The Deivers have the most wonderful library!" She held up a book. "Do you think she'd let me borrow one?"

"I don't see why not." I smiled.

Considering that the family would be coming home to a house with three bodies in the basement, I'd think that would be the least of their concerns.

We went next door to the billiard room, where Stacey and Juliette were involved in a game of pool.

"Cool!" the girls shouted as they each ran to a side of the table.

Stacey smiled. "Do you girls want to know how to play?"

To my surprise, Juliette nodded and handed out pool cues. Maybe a couple of murders had dimmed her fury. Now I'd have to kill someone any time I was around her—but still, this was an improvement.

Four squeals erupted as the girls grasped their cues. Soo Jin and I slipped out of the room before they could change their minds. This was a good idea. We could move faster, and since the other two people we were looking for were killers, it was safer for the girls.

We hit the conservatory, ballroom, kitchen, and dining room before finding ourselves back in the lounge with Dennis, who'd somehow discovered an apple pie and was eating the whole thing.

"What?" he asked. "Miriam said I could have it."

"Miriam's back?" Soo Jin asked.

He nodded, and we heard a clatter in the kitchen. We raced to the room but found it empty.

"I'm getting tired of this," I grumbled with a look outside. It was still storming, but not raining as hard. I winked at Soo Jin. "Fancy a walk to the cottage?"

As we stepped outside for only the second time in twenty-four hours, we could see broken tree branches littering the yard. The temperature had dropped, and a chill wind howled. But the rain had let up a bit.

"Let's make this quick," Soo Jin said as she ran down the steps.

We turned right and ran along the side of the house, turning the corner to see the cottage. The ground wasn't as swampy, but it looked like there was another way in around back. While it wasn't dry, it wasn't that muddy either. We took it and walked around the cottage to find a door on the other side.

It was open. I knocked as I went in and called out for Miriam and Ned. We found ourselves in a cozy little sitting room with two comfy chairs and a fireplace. The building was narrow, so we had to walk through a bathroom to get to the bedroom. The two beds were freshly made, and the house was neat as a pin. Unfortunately, it was also empty.

"Do you think they're using the secret passages to get around?" Soo Jin asked as we went back to the entrance and outside.

I gave her a look. "You don't think Caroline and Wren have them, do you?"

"Why would they bother with the staff?" Soo Jin asked.

"Maybe they saw something that they shouldn't." I took off back to the house.

We ran up onto the porch and into the hall entryway. We barely made it before a huge downpour hit, followed by large hail.

"We didn't check upstairs," Soo Jin said.

As we walked toward the staircase, we were met by a grisly site. That niggling thing missing from Taylor's room revealed itself. At the bottom of the steps, clad in the scarlet outfit that Taylor wore when she'd arrived, was the broken body of Wren Gable.

CHAPTER ELEVEN

Soo Jin checked for a pulse, but I already knew the woman's neck had been broken. I'd seen injuries like that before. Well, assassiny injuries. The medical examiner shook her head and then ran into the dining room and returned with the tablecloth, which she draped over the body.

Which was smart because just then Stacey and Juliette and four little girls came around from the other side of the staircase.

"We heard a scream," Stacey said, unable to take her eyes off the lump beneath the tablecloth. "Is that…"

I nodded. "Wren Gable. Can you go get Dennis and head to the library with everyone? The Kasinskis are there."

The girls turned to go with her, but Betty lingered long enough to perform an impressive martial arts move using a pool cue as a bo staff. She spun the rod without looking at it, ending with it under her arm. Then with a wink to us, she ran off and joined them too.

"Caroline!" I said tightly as I sprang up the stairs. "Stay with the body," I told Soo Jin.

Since I didn't hear footfalls on the steps behind me, I knew Soo Jin had stayed behind. I took the steps two at a time until I reached the top. Had Caroline decided it was time for Wren to go? Maybe it was because of Wren's comment about the killers this morning. Maybe she'd always planned to kill her. Or maybe she just had a chance to do it. Rex once told me that many murders were simply crimes of opportunity. The killer saw an opening and ran with it. Was that what happened here?

Either way, it didn't matter. I was going to find that woman and take her out once and for all. I searched every room, bathroom, and closet as I came across them. When at last I came to Caroline's room, it was empty. I retraced my steps, hitting every room again.

Caroline wasn't on the second floor.

I ran down the steps, and Soo Jin looked up at me. She spotted the question on my face and shook her head.

"Caroline, Miriam, and Ned are missing," I said as I doubled over to catch my breath.

"Or they're using the secret passageways," Soo Jin added.

"Do you think the three of them are in on it?" I hadn't thought of that. It seemed unlikely.

I sighed and sat down on the bottom step. If I kept this up, we'd be at it all night. That would be a phenomenal waste of energy, and I didn't have any to spare.

"Miriam gave Dennis the pie," Soo Jin said. "Which means they're here somewhere."

"Either Caroline killed them both, or they're helping her," I mused.

Soo Jin nodded at the tablecloth. "And look what she does to people who help her."

Now we had an interesting dilemma. The rest of the guests, the girls, and Council employees were in the library. The body in front of us needed examination and moving. Miriam, Ned, and Caroline were missing. If I left Soo Jin here alone to examine the body, I'd be putting her in danger.

Then again, the people in the library weren't necessarily safe if Caroline decided to take a shortcut and mow everyone down with a machine gun. And I had no idea what the staff was up to or where they were.

Soo Jin watched me struggle. "Go to the library and send Juliette here to assist me. Leave the girls with the Kasinskis, Dennis, and Stacey, and that gives you time to get the murder board out of our room and set it up in the library."

I clapped my hands together. "Good thinking. We can ask the others if they have any ideas. The murder board might jog their memories."

After installing Juliette with Soo Jin, I ran upstairs and threw all the supplies into a backpack and grabbed the Clue board and easel. I set up everything in the library.

Filling the group in on Wren's death was hard, but hardly surprising, as the guests nodded numbly.

"What's that?" Violet's voice quavered a little when she saw the board with its Post-it bodies.

Arthur put his arm around her.

"It's a murder board," Lauren explained as she took a little paper Wren, tore and bent the arms and legs askew, and placed it at the foot of the stairs.

"It'll help us get answers," Betty said, still holding the pool cue menacingly. She launched into a set of drills that would make a black belt envious.

I took the pool cue out of her hands and set it aside. Then I took Post-its for everyone still living and moved them to where they'd been at the time Wren was murdered. Arthur's and Violet's went into the library. Dennis's went into the lounge. Stacey, Juliette, and one large one for the girls went into the billiard room. I placed one for me and Soo Jin outside on the porch. Since there wasn't a porch on the game board, I stuck them next to the board.

Caroline, Miriam, and Ned's paper people were placed in the hall entryway, since we had no idea where they were at the time of Wren's murder.

"I have some questions," I started.

Ava and Inez stepped forward and started smacking their fists into their hands. They looked like little mafia henchmen, backing me up. I waved them away, and they grudgingly sat down.

"Has anyone seen Wren—alive—or Caroline and Miriam or Ned since breakfast?"

The Kasinskis looked at each other in confusion. Dennis chewed his lip, and Stacey shook her head. Dennis reminded me about the pie. From the crumbs on his shirt, it looked like he'd eaten the whole thing.

"Okay," I tried again. "When you all left the dining room, did anyone see where Caroline and Wren went?"

Violet's eyes lit up, and she raised her hand. "I saw them at the foot of the stairs. They seemed to be arguing." She turned to her husband. "Right, Arthur?"

Arthur nodded. "We went to the library and got books and sat down to read. I never saw anything after that."

"Nobody walked past the doorway?" Soo Jin asked.

The couple shook their heads. Violet seemed to remember something. "I saw Stacey and Juliette in the billiard room. The doors are across from each other."

"How about you, Dennis? Did you see Wren and Caroline?"

He shrugged. "I heard them arguing, but not well enough to hear it. I didn't see them."

The lounge was kitty-corner across from the stairs. I nodded at Lauren, and she moved Caroline to the steps next to the bent and twisted Wren paper doll. Three people remembered hearing or seeing Caroline and Wren near the stairs. Did they go upstairs? Wren had Taylor's dress on, and she wasn't wearing it for breakfast, so they must have. Well, at least Wren had.

I wished the three missing people would show up so we could get their stories—even if I didn't expect Caroline to out herself as the killer.

"Let's assume Wren went upstairs." I nodded at Lauren, and she moved the Post-it body up to the top of the stairs on the board. "Where she put on Taylor's dress."

"Are you saying Dr. Regent killed her?" Dennis's eyes grew round.

Yes. "No, I'm not. Not until we have all the facts. I just wish I knew where they were right now so I could…"

That was when Caroline walked into the room. She found a chair in the corner and dragged it toward the rest of us, who, I was sure, were wearing odd expressions. She looked at all of us staring at her and seemed to be annoyed. She turned her attention to the murder board and frowned.

"Okay," she said slowly. "What did I miss?"

CHAPTER TWELVE

I was the first to recover from the shock of seeing her. "Where have you been? We were looking for you!"

Caroline leaned back in her chair. "I got bored, so I walked around, exploring this floor. I even went out on the porch for a bit."

"We were on the porch, and we didn't see you," I said.

The doctor shrugged. "It's a big porch. We must've just missed each other."

"No one," I insisted, "has seen you since you were arguing with Wren after breakfast."

All eyes turned back to the main suspect.

Caroline studied the medical examiner. "What are you talking about? I wasn't arguing with her. Where is she? She'll tell you."

How could she miss the body covered with a tablecloth at the foot of the stairs? She'd have to have walked right past it to get in here.

"Wren was murdered a short time ago," Soo Jin said levelly.

"You just walked past her," Dennis said. "She's at the foot of the stairs."

Caroline's jaw dropped. "I came from the kitchen, past the ballroom, and into here through the side door. I didn't walk past the stairs."

Then why wasn't she rushing out to see the body? She was a doctor, after all. And if Wren was her friend, why wouldn't she want to confirm what we'd said? But no, Caroline stayed put.

"Did you go upstairs at any time?" I asked.

She shook her head. "No. I was on this level the whole time." The woman looked around her, and something dawned on her. "Am I a suspect?"

"I'm afraid so, dear," Violet said softly. "Everyone's a suspect."

Caroline's face grew red. "I'm not a killer. I didn't kill Wren or anyone else!"

"I say"—Betty stepped forward with the pool cue she'd mysteriously retrieved—"you let me take the poop doctor outside for a few minutes."

A tremendous thunderclap boomed, making everyone jump.

"You can't prove I did it, can you?" Caroline said defiantly.

"We can put you near the scene of the crime, and I think you have motive enough for all three of the murders," I said.

She looked puzzled. "What are you talking about?"

"You and Taylor were close friends until you had a falling out and she started seeing Thad," Ava said, ticking the victims off using her fingers. Huh. I didn't know she'd been listening. "That's why you killed Taylor and Thad."

Caroline shook her head. "That's ridiculous. And even if it was true, why would I kill Enos and Wren? I just met them yesterday!"

Betty growled, "That sounds like something the killer would say!" She gave a karate cry that sounded like a high-pitched *Owwweeeoh* and twirled the pool cue in front of her.

Ava looked at me expectantly. It was time to lay out my theory.

"Enos was a red herring," I said. "You and Wren were working together. You killed Taylor, and she killed Thad. Then you killed Wren to silence her."

Dr. Regent folded her arms over her chest. "How do you know Wren didn't just fall down the stairs?"

It was odd how there was no protestation of innocence, just a challenge to my deduction skills. I found it interesting and damning at the same time.

Soo Jin stepped forward. "Because I found bruises on her upper back consistent with handprints. She was pushed. Just like the poem said—one fell down some stairs."

Caroline blanched. Either she didn't know that, or she'd pushed her.

"Face it," Ava said. "You're Kevin. As a doctor you have access to whatever poisoned Enos!"

"Who's Kevin?" Caroline asked. "What are you talking about?"

Betty sighed and pulled the poem out of her pocket. "Kevin the Killer. From the poem. You're Kevin. Duh."

The doctor looked at me with confusion in her eyes.

"Kevin," I said slowly. "From the poem. Eight little Girl Scouts on a trip with Kevin. You're Kevin."

Caroline shook her head. "Um…I don't…"

Inez interrupted her. "You were the only one to see Taylor leave the room last night."

"And you said the killings were over at breakfast." Arthur put his two cents in.

Violet nodded in agreement.

Caroline listened to all this with a poker face to rival an Easter Island statue. We all waited for the confession that had to come next, which would soon be followed by tying her to a chair. Maybe I could let the girls do it. They were getting very good at knots.

"I didn't do it," she snapped. "Any of it. And you can't prove I did."

She had us there. We only had circumstantial evidence at best. Soo Jin came the closest to scientific evidence, but without a lab, she couldn't do much.

"Yes we can!" Inez shouted. "The poison could be in her room!"

I hadn't thought of that. "Stay here!" I told everyone. "Soo Jin, with me!"

"You can't go through my room without a search warrant!" Caroline exploded as she jumped up and came within inches of me.

I stepped even closer, hoping she'd take a swing. "Yes I can. And I will." And then I ran up the stairs.

Behind me, I heard Stacey and Violet tell the girls to stay put, but Caroline and Dennis were hot on my tail. We bounded the steps, almost abreast. Caroline surged at the top of the stairs and threw her body between me and her door.

"You," she growled. "Are not going in there."

I turned toward Wren's room and gasped. "Oh wow! Is that a clue?"

It was all I needed. Caroline slipped a little to her right to crane her neck, and using a pressure point in her armpit, I tossed her aside and went into the room. What I saw made me gasp in shock.

"This is the messiest room I've ever seen!"

Clothes were scattered everywhere, on every surface, including the floor. Caroline charged me, but Dennis pulled her arms behind her and gave me a nod. I wondered if sudden activity had hurt him.

Soo Jin and I went through the closet and dresser and checked the bathroom. We lifted clothes and looked under them and checked every inch of the room while Caroline fumed. I'd love to say we found a wrench or lead pipe covered in blood or a bottle labelled CYANIDE or even a tub of lube, but I couldn't because we didn't.

Caroline's room was clean. Well, figuratively at least.

I was just considering checking all the rooms, when I heard Ned shout "LUNCH" from the bottom of the stairs. We could continue searching later. Right now, I needed to talk to those two.

Dennis grabbed Caroline's arm and shoved. Where had this guy come from? Up until now the only thing he'd assaulted was an apple pie—and from the looks of things, the pie didn't make it.

The dining room was laid out with six large pizzas. That was a surprise, and a concern because that was my weakness. The girls had already started digging in, staying at their kiddie table in the corner, even though there was now room for all of them at the big table.

The other guests sat and began to tear into the food. We all kept an eye on Caroline, even though there was really nowhere she could go. The storm was waning, but we were on a very small island with no boat. I snagged the pizza cutter so it couldn't be used as a weapon. It wasn't very sharp, but it was a good idea to operate on the safe side.

Oh sure, you probably think you can't kill anyone with a dull pizza cutter. I once witnessed an Italian police officer injure and disable four burglars, armed only with a rolling pizza cutter. Hint—it's all in the wrist.

"Ned!" I called out toward the kitchen, where I hoped he still was. "Can I see you and Miriam for a moment, please?"

The groundskeeper appeared and didn't look too happy about it. "I was in the hall. She should be in the kitchen."

Soo Jin and I followed him into the kitchen, where Miriam was washing up. None of the other guests followed us. Maybe they thought we had it covered. Maybe their attention spans were shot. Whatever it was, I was hoping there'd still be pizza left when I got back.

"Where have you two been all morning?" I asked.

The two looked at each other and then back at me.

"What do you mean?" Ned asked.

"I mean, you guys have been missing since breakfast." I pointed at Soo Jin. "We've looked everywhere for you, even searching your cottage. Couldn't find you anywhere," I said evenly. "So I'll ask again. Where were you?"

"None of your business!" he snapped.

Miriam nodded in agreement.

"I'm afraid it is my business," I said. "Didn't you see Wren's body at the foot of the stairs when you called for lunch?"

The man's face froze. He looked totally confused. "I didn't go to the stairs to call you. I did it from the dining room door. Another one of you is dead? Seriously? What kind of fundraiser is this?"

I nodded. "It doesn't look good that you two have been gone. It's storming outside. Where could you have been?"

Miriam burst into tears. She was so quiet I could only tell she was upset by the water pouring over her cheeks.

"There, there, it's alright, kiddo." Ned wrapped his arms around her.

"Kiddo?" I asked.

"She's my daughter," Ned responded. "You didn't know that?"

I shook my head. "I suspected as much, but I wasn't sure. But it still doesn't explain where you two were."

"In the shed," Miriam sobbed. "Sorting the pantry in there for lunch and dinner."

I remembered seeing a small building when we ran back to the cottage. It was big enough to be a room. Was that where they'd been?

"What do you know about Dr. Caroline Regent?" Soo Jin asked.

"The gruff one?" Ned asked as he released his daughter, who was now hiccupping softly. "Never seen her before."

"Okay," I said before turning on my heel and heading across the hall to the dining room.

"That's it?" Soo Jin caught up with me. "That's all you're going to ask?"

"It's lunch, and they aren't going anywhere until the boat comes back," I answered. "And most importantly, you can't solve crime on an empty stomach."

As we walked into the dining room, Soo Jin whispered, "I suppose not. But I hope yours is strong, because after this, we're going to search the bodies for clues."

She sat down and grabbed a slice as I just stood there, jaw on the floor. I'd seen plenty of dead bodies before but never an autopsy. Was that what she was planning? I sat down, stuffed the pizza roller under my chair, put that idea out of my mind, and started to eat.

Sure, we didn't find any evidence in Caroline's room. So what? She was still my main suspect. As long as we kept an eye on her, we should be okay. Right?

I looked at my troop, eating and talking among themselves, and felt terrible about how this weekend turned out. Which was silly, since it was more likely that they thought this was the greatest weekend of their lives. I wondered what their teachers would think on Monday when they told their respective classes about four dead bodies, a villainous poop doctor, and a drowning in a bowl of lube. We probably wouldn't be able to hold meetings at the school anymore.

The whole thing went off script right from the start. And we'd had a great event planned. Linda Willard had outdone herself with the storyline and script. Dennis would die (not really) first, followed by Violet (again, not really) and Caroline (this should make sense by now).

Thad was supposed to play the part of the killer. And look how that turned out for him. It was going to be fun, with no blood or gore and a fake autopsy or two. Now, we had four bodies (dead for real this time) and a real autopsy coming up.

I was super impressed with my girls. They didn't fall apart at the murders or go to pieces with the storm. They were tough, smart, tenacious kids, and I was lucky to have them. Granted, they'd escaped out the window to burgle the conservatory last night, and Betty was starting to scare me with that pool cue, but on the whole, they came through with cool heads and nerves of steel. Most grown-ups would crumble under these circumstances.

Kelly would probably disagree. She'd felt that the girls had become numb to murder since being around me. Even though none of the murders that happened in my presence were my fault, she might have had a point.

Most kids weren't exposed to this kind of thing unless they lived in war-torn third-world countries, inner-city Chicago, or one very disturbing, wealthy suburb in Montevideo. By the way, never ever go there. Never.

Was I doing the wrong thing? It's not like I had any choice this time since we were trapped in this house in the middle of a lake with no hope for rescue anytime soon.

No. They'd be okay. I didn't have any degrees in psychology or elementary education (my real degree in Russian with a minor in Japanese history seemed a little useless here), but my troop was amazing. They were leaders who weren't afraid of things that go bump in the night. The least I could do was help them grow.

No one spoke during lunch. Caroline glared at everyone, including the girls. The rest were on edge, suspicious of Doctor Death but afraid it might not be her and there could still be more bodies before we were through.

I knew that my girls and Soo Jin were innocent. Did the guests think otherwise? I did have a past based on violence. My CIA record was getting out, and then there was Lana.

Lana! I'd totally forgotten about her. A terrible thought popped into my head, causing my blood to run cold. Could she be the killer? I wouldn't put it past her. Dennis knew her—which was bizarre because he certainly wasn't her type. Why did she groom him, and how did she know he was going to be with me this weekend?

While I mostly didn't think Lana was really the killer, she had been in my mind these last several months to the point I thought she was following me. Rex and Riley, my former handler, thought I was crazy. When this was over, and if he was still alive, I'd be grilling Dennis on his "relationship" with Lana. And then I'd use him as bait to draw her out of whatever hole she was hiding in.

Argh! This was not productive. I had to shove all thoughts of her aside. Right now I had to focus on this problem and only this problem. There would be no more dead bodies for the rest of our imprisonment on Penny Island. Not as long as I could keep Caroline in my sights. I didn't know for sure that she was the killer, but she was my main suspect, and I wasn't taking any chances.

Lunch ended with everyone retreating to the hallway outside the dining room. The mood was as overcast as the sky.

"Look!" Violet shouted as she pointed to the windows in the dining room. "It's stopped raining!"

"Can we go outside?" Ava begged. "Please?"

Of course they wanted out. They'd been cooped up in here for the past twenty-four hours with a killer. Something in the back of my mind told me this wasn't a good idea. But I was so sleep deprived and murder saturated, I couldn't put my finger on it.

"Let's do!" Violet smiled at the girls and Arthur. "It will be safe if we all go together."

I looked around and saw hopeful faces…except for Caroline, who was still angry with me.

"Okay. But just onto the porch, okay?" What was it I was forgetting? Something was off.

The girls were gone before I could finish. The rest of us ran after them, and soon we were all standing on the porch. The clouds were definitely menacing, and lightning flickered among them. We weren't out of the woods yet.

Caroline was in my peripheral vision on my right, with everyone else on my left. I just needed to make sure I knew where she was at all times. Like I'd said earlier, she couldn't get far if she ran. I was just too tired to run after her.

Arthur's eyes were closed as he took deep breaths. Dennis even smiled. Stacey and Juliette relaxed a little. Everyone knew that no one had been killed in public. The killer worked in the shadows.

The killer…that was it. Something about the killer and his plans. Wait, the poem! Wren had "fallen down some stairs" like in the poem. In my rush to find the killer, I'd deviated from the one declaration the killer had made. The poem was the manifesto…the script for the remaining murders. I'd almost forgotten that.

Violet carefully took the steps down to the sidewalk. She seemed almost giddy to be outside. Somehow, we'd have to make this up to the Kasinskis. They were the only donors who didn't want refunds for the disastrous weekend.

What was the next line? What number were we on? I counted the murders. Four. The next murder would rhyme with *four*, like the others.

The elderly woman spun around and looked up into the sky.

CRAAAAACK!

One was crushed by a branch! And there was Violet, under a tree! We'd walked right into it!

"Inside!" I shouted. That wasn't lightning. The huge branch hanging over Violet had started to break. And the old woman was about to be crushed.

Lunging off the deck, I tackled Violet and rolled the two of us out of the way as the huge branch fell onto the ground. The earth shook. It had to be three feet in diameter, and it just missed her!

"Are you alright?" I helped her to her feet. "I'm so sorry!"

She nodded weakly, her face ashen. "I'm okay, thanks to your quick thinking." She was unsteady on her feet, and I took her arm to help her. "Thank you."

Arthur cried out as he came down the steps and gathered his petite wife into his arms. I searched the faces on the porch. Each and every person seemed surprised. Then I examined the broken edge of the branch.

"Get everyone inside," I shouted while motioning for Soo Jin to join me. When the door closed, I pointed to the branch. "It's a clean cut," I said as she knelt to examine it. "Someone cut that branch and tried to kill Violet."

I turned to face the door. "We need to get the poem. The killer isn't through with the rest of us."

CHAPTER THIRTEEN

Something gleamed on the other side of the branch as huge droplets started to fall from the sky. I straddled it, studying the torn wood. It was some sort of saw/wire, about an inch thick in diameter.

I followed it to find one end nailed to the tree while the other end just hung there. Unless I missed my guess, I'd say the other end had been tied to the bannister…right where Caroline had been standing.

"We need to get back inside," Soo Jin shouted.

The rain was coming faster and harder. We just couldn't catch a break. There would be no rescue today. How was it possible that it rained this long? It was like the killer conspired with the weather so we could all be hunted.

As we walked into the house, anger washed over me. Thad and Taylor were a bad sort. Wren was annoying, and Enos was…well…there. But Violet was a nice little old lady. This had to stop. Now.

What was the solution? Tie Caroline to a chair and beat a confession out of her? She'd sure acted strangely when accused.

"Mrs. Wrath!" screamed four girls in unison from the lounge.

We ran inside to find the girls standing around the table with the figures. I'd forgotten all about them. When Wren was murdered, I should've checked. Now, there were only three figurines left.

No, wait, that wasn't right. Two looked like the others, but one was new. An action figure of some sort. Which meant that the killer took one of the figurines and replaced it with this doll.

"She looks like you!" Inez said.

"She's right!" Soo Jin gasped.

The doll had short, curly dirty blonde hair and was wearing some sort of jacket over a T-shirt. I picked it up and examined it. The T-shirt read, *Property of the CIA.*

"Don't you remember the last line of the poem?" Betty nodded. "You're the last one."

"But that can't be right!" Inez mumbled. "There are two figurines here and the doll. But there are four guests left, Arthur, Violet, Dennis, and Caroline."

"The killer didn't put one on there for themselves because they knew they weren't going to die," Lauren reasoned.

"But two new ones are broken." Inez pointed.

She was right. One for Wren and one for Violet. But the killer acted prematurely. They hadn't counted on me or anyone else being there to save her.

"Why are you smiling?" Soo Jin asked.

"Because…" I grinned. "The killer made a mistake. For the first time, they screwed up." And that was a good sign.

"At least we know Stacey and Juliette are safe," Soo Jin said. "I think they should watch over the girls and the Kasinskis while we take Wren and Thad to the basement for autopsies."

"But the murderer is now killing people in front of everyone else." I shook my head. "I don't know if anyone is safe right now."

Soo Jin put her hands on her hips. "We don't have any evidence. We can't exactly lock her up without proof. That's just asking for a lawsuit when this is over."

"I have no problem locking her up without proof," I said. "In fact, I'm kind of thinking of waterboarding her for a confession. It would be quicker."

"Merry Wrath!" Soo Jin startled me by shouting. "We are going to do this by the book—like civilized people. And the one thing I know how to do is all we have right now."

Soo Jin had never been mad at anyone or anything for as long as I'd known her. This normally bouncy, bubbly person was losing it. It made sense—witnessing one murder after another was nerve-racking at best—even for someone who spent all their time cutting up dead people. And I knew she was right, because I was one of those people who needed to have the voice of reason kicked into her every now and then.

I sighed. "Okay. Let's get this over with."

After settling everyone in the conservatory—just to get them all in a different room—I got Violet a glass of brandy from the lounge and with a quick glare at Caroline told them I'd be right back.

I wasn't sure how long this would take, and I didn't tell them what we were doing, because I didn't want Caroline to think she had time to finish Violet off. Before I left, I approached the doctor and whispered one or two extremely violent threats in her ear. Once she blanched appropriately, I joined Soo Jin in the hallway.

Thad was still upstairs, and as we were both exhausted, we decided he should stay there. Soo Jin uncovered him, and I watched from the doorway, where I'd insisted I needed to be a lookout. The medical examiner pulled a lamp down from the nightstand and angled the shade to give her more light. Then she probed the inside of Thad's mouth and nose.

As I averted my eyes, I tried to think of a way to confine Caroline. Searching her room wasn't legal, but we didn't find anything anyway. I really wanted to chain her up but knew that since I wasn't a police officer, she'd have a strong legal case for a lawsuit. This could be a citizen's arrest thingy, but I wasn't sure how that worked.

We still had the afternoon and evening…with the dire possibility of being stuck here overnight again. No one on shore would miss us until lunchtime tomorrow because that was when we told the boat to come back.

"Merry?" Soo Jin stood up and ran into the bathroom to wash her hands.

"All done?" I peeked and saw that she'd covered the body back up.

Soo Jin emerged, wiping her hands on a towel. "He suffocated. The blow on the head wasn't enough to kill him. And I have the distinct feeling that the killer wanted him alive so they could smother him in the lubricant."

"Did you find anything else?" I asked.

"Not really, unless you consider that for an idiot, he had eclectic reading material." She pointed to a book on the other nightstand.

I picked it up. "*The Canterbury Tales*? Seriously?"

Was Thad smarter than we had given him credit?

"Maybe they only have the classics in the library?" I asked.

Soo Jin shook her head. "The girls found Agatha Christie and Nancy Drew books. Maybe he just liked Chaucer?"

Thad didn't strike me as the type to read fourteenth-century English literature. But I couldn't think of another reason why this book would be here, and I couldn't ask the man, so I dropped it. Besides, it was time to check his wife. And the sooner these autopsies were done, the better.

At the bottom of the stairs, I stood guard as Soo Jin pulled back the tablecloth.

"I'd prefer to look her over here," she said. "Make sure no one comes near. Then we can move her and Thad downstairs with the others."

"Okay," I said a little too quickly.

Music from a piano came from the conservatory, with voices singing Girl Scout songs. My girls loved to sing, and I appreciated whoever was playing piano for giving everyone a nice distraction.

"Her neck was broken during the fall," Soo Jin muttered behind me.

"Are you avoiding medical examiner terminology because I don't understand it?" I tried to joke.

She giggled. "Sorry. I just thought that was easier."

"You said she'd been pushed. That there were handprints on her back?" I remembered.

"Oh. Right. I made that up."

I whirled around to stare at her. "You did what?" Soo Jin didn't strike me as a liar. I liked it!

She nodded as she started to unzip the back of Wren's, or rather, Taylor's dress. "I'm pretty sure that's what we'll find. I wanted to put Caroline on the spot." She peered under the dress. "Yup, contusions. That's what happened alright." She looked up at me. "It takes a while for the blood to drain to the part of her that's facedown. That's when you see the bruising best."

I shrugged. "Works for me."

We lifted the woman and carried her down the stairs to the basement, putting her with Enos's and Taylor's remains. Then we collected Thad's remains and moved him downstairs. After a quick dash up the stairs to the conservatory to make sure things were okay, we returned to the basement.

"Where'd you get that?" I pointed at the huge lamp Soo Jin had in her hands.

"From the conservatory. I need it down here. The light isn't very good."

I fidgeted as she set things up. Hopefully, she didn't have a scalpel on her. Blood doesn't bother me, but there was something about these murders that creeped me out. Especially after the very public attack on Violet.

The murderer took a huge risk trying to kill the elderly woman in front of all of us. Why did they do it? And would they try again since this one failed? Was Violet Kasinski in danger of another attempt?

The remaining clues in the poem popped into my head. Someone was going to die from sniffing glue, another would be roasted in the sun, and then I…well, it didn't say how I was going to be killed.

In fact, none of the other clues indicated who the next victims would be. I was fairly certain it would be Dennis and Arthur. And possibly another attempt on Violet's life. Would she stick with the modus operandi being "crushed by a branch"? Well, from here on out, I was going to stick to my number one suspect—Caroline.

The continued murders confused me. Caroline knew I suspected her. Either she didn't care anymore and the murders were the most important thing to her, or she was trying to cast doubt on my suspicions.

What would I do if I were her? Besides getting a makeover and trying to have a little fun now and then. We weren't exactly the same person. Would I give up or keep going? I suppose I would do whatever I thought would confuse the police when they got here.

She really got lucky. The weather certainly helped her. Did she know a horrendous storm was going to hit? If the weather had been nice, we would've called the sheriff right away and Thad, Taylor, and Wren would still be alive.

What about Ned and Miriam? Caroline was my main suspect, but could I rule them completely out? Those two had behaved strangely throughout the weekend. Were they involved? Were they related to Caroline? Had they joined forces?

There was a scurrying sound behind the walls. Gertrude. She was the smartest one of all of us. Hiding in the walls was the best way to stay safe. If only I could hide the girls there. Of course, then the only thing we'd hear was four girls squealing and chasing down the Holland lop.

The bunny appeared next to me. I didn't even care where she'd come from. She hopped over to the bodies and sniffed.

"Would you grab her?" Soo Jin asked. "She's getting in the way."

I gently lifted the rabbit and held her in my arms. She responded by sniffing me. Gertrude really was cute. I stroked her ears, and she settled and closed her eyes.

"Good bunny," I said. "I'll bet you know who did it. You probably saw some of the murders. Too bad we can't put you on the witness stand."

Gertrude responded by gently nibbling on my shirt. I didn't even know bunnies were good pets. What would Philby think if I brought a rabbit home? This animal was almost as big as the feline fuhrer. Philby loved tormenting Rex's dog, Leonard. Would she do the same to a bunny? Looking at the size of the lop's claws and feet, I'd say she was armed well enough.

"I can't find any other clues on Thad." Soo Jin sighed as she sat back on her heels. "I stand by my original theory that he was bludgeoned and suffocated."

"What about the others?" I set Gertrude down and pointed at the other three bodies. The rabbit skittered away and soon was out of sight.

"Give me a few more minutes." She winked. "I might find something yet."

Soo Jin turned to Wren. She unzipped Taylor's dress again, and I saw two hand-sized bruises on her back. She was definitely pushed.

"Was she bludgeoned beforehand? Like Thad?"

Soo Jin shook her head. "No, but her neck is broken from the fall down the stairs."

We had no gloves, which I knew would be better. But Dr. Body touched as little as she could, using one finger to gently search the dead woman's hands.

"No skin in the fingernails or broken fingernails." She shook her head. "Wren didn't fight back. Which means she didn't see it coming. Just like Thad and Taylor—no defensive injuries."

"Our killer wanted to get it over with quickly. They were caught unawares." I frowned. "Why wouldn't they want them to see them before they struck? Wouldn't the killer want the victims to know who it was?"

Soo Jin shrugged. "Not necessarily. Not if they wanted to get back to the lounge or out of Thad's room unseen."

"Huh. Seems like an opportunity missed." If I wanted someone dead, I'd make sure they at least saw me.

"The killer had quick instincts, grabbing every opportunity as it came up," Soo Jin said as she probed Wren's pockets. "It would've been easy to put poison in Enos's food. Especially with the first meal since there were so many of us there. And when attention was drawn to the opposite end of the table, the killer pounced."

I snapped my fingers. "Taylor slipped off on her own. Caroline knew that because Taylor told her. She could've been watching for that and jumped to it."

"And Thad sent Wren downstairs. That was an opportunity to kill him." Soo Jin nodded.

"Unless Wren was in on it," I mused. "We still haven't ruled that out."

Soo Jin sighed. "I doubt I'll find any evidence of that." She frowned and pulled something out of Wren's pocket. "What's this?"

I leaned in. "It looks like a page from a book."

The torn piece of paper came from a corner, but not the place where a page number would be, and there was nothing on it. I took it from her and pocketed it. Maybe I could compare it to Thad's book. I wasn't sure why it would matter if a page from Thad's book ended up in his wife's possession. Although technically it was in Taylor's dress pocket. Was it some sort of code to meet up later? But then again, Taylor had changed out of the dress by the time she'd slipped off to the study.

My head was starting to spin, and my nerves were on edge. Hopefully, the rest of these "autopsies" would produce some solid evidence so we could tie Caroline up for the night and get some rest.

As Soo Jin moved on to Taylor, I picked up the trophy, in its bag, that had gone through her neck. It really was a fencing trophy for first place in the state. That was so like the dead woman, who was big on being the first in everything.

"This is meaningful," I said. "The killer made a point of using a first-place trophy."

Soo Jin nodded. "I just wish I had the weapon that bludgeoned Thad."

"Or the bottle of poison for Enos." I sighed.

"Wouldn't that be great?" She gave me a weak smile. "I'd love it if my job were so easy. Sadly, killers rarely leave a *How I Did It* manifesto behind."

"That would make things easier."

She pointed at the body. "Everything is consistent with being stabbed in the throat. The trophy hit her jugular vein. Taylor was dead in seconds."

Soo Jin moved on to Enos, and I set the trophy down. These modes of murder puzzled me. If the killer didn't care if the victims knew who was killing them, why go to all this trouble with the poem, the trophy, the lube, and Wren wearing Taylor's dress? Was it just for her own personal satisfaction?

I felt like I was missing something. The killer was making a statement to the rest of us, not to the victims. It seemed backwards to me, but wasn't she telling us that there was a reason why each person was killed? And if that was the case, why make it so cryptic?

"That's interesting," Soo Jin mumbled. She was bent over Enos's neck and had pulled up her cell phone's flashlight app.

I stepped closer. "What is it?"

"A needle mark." She sat up and stared at the body, lost in thought.

"He wasn't poisoned through the food…" I mumbled.

She shook her head and smiled. "I think someone administered the poison with a hypodermic needle."

My mind turned back to lunch yesterday. Betty approached him. I didn't remember anyone else. And I was sure Betty hadn't killed him. Ninety-nine to one, but mostly sure.

"In the back of his neck," Soo Jin mused. "But cyanide works instantaneously. Caroline would've had to be standing behind him, and Enos might've cried out when it was administered."

"You said cyanide works immediately," I wondered aloud. "So she couldn't have done it in the lounge or on the way into the dining room."

"Unless it's something else," She thought about this. "It could be from a previous doctor's visit, or he was doing drugs. Although, very few junkies shoot up in the back of the neck. Too hard to reach." She demonstrated by trying to inject herself in the back of the neck with an imaginary hypodermic needle.

"Great," I grumped. "It made sense when we thought the food had been poisoned."

"It could've been the fish." She looked at the plate of food in the baggie. "I just don't have any way of knowing without my lab."

"If Caroline's the killer, do you think she'll go after Violet again?"

Soo Jin seemed frustrated. "I think it's time we tied her up or something. We can't run that risk."

"I know. We have to do something. But I don't want to feed her by hand or untie her when she needs to go to the bathroom. Maybe we can lock her in her room?"

We joined the group, still huddling in the conservatory. The girls were playing a board game. Caroline and Arthur were reading, with Arthur glaring at the doctor every now and then. Dennis was napping at the other end of the room on one of the three sofas. Violet was intently watching the girls. Stacey and

Juliette had placed chairs on either side of the door, presumably to guard who went in and out.

"The lightning has stopped." Betty looked up as we walked in.

"Yeah, but it's still raining like crazy." Ava kept her eyes on her cards.

I didn't recognize the game, but I was too lost in thought to ask. Soo Jin sat down next to the girls, and I sat down next to Violet.

"How are you feeling?" I asked.

"Oh, I'm fine. Just a little scare, that's all. I'm sure it was an accident. There were a lot of tree branches down outside."

Caroline smirked until she saw the look on my face, and went back to her book.

The figurine had been broken, probably in advance. But if Violet wanted to believe it was an accident, I was willing to pretend. Why put any more stress on the woman?

As for ideas—I was out. Soo Jin was right. We should lock Caroline up. But wouldn't it be better to watch her like a hawk and maybe even catch her in the act? Maybe that was too dangerous.

We sat in the conservatory, everyone lost in their own little worlds, until Ned walked in.

"Dinner will be ready soon," he growled and left.

The adults nodded listlessly. No one was much in the mood for food, but going through the motions on a routine might help. People were comforted by what they were familiar with. As for me, I could always eat.

I picked up a magazine from the coffee table and pretended to look through it, glancing furtively at Caroline now and then. If she noticed, she didn't react. A wave of exhaustion crashed over me.

Wow. I hadn't realized how tired I was. But then, I hadn't gotten much sleep the night before. My brain was running on adrenaline that gave up the ghost hours ago. If there was a hamster running inside my head on a wheel, he'd have been dead by morning.

What were the Deivers going to think when they returned home to find bodies in the basement, blood on the carpet, and their trophy confiscated? And what would the Girl Scout Council think when they found out that half of their big donors had been killed?

Then again, maybe these people put the Council in their estate planning. I stifled a giggle, thinking of the Girl Scouts having a team of assassins who knocked off people to collect from their wills. Stacey would be the perfect assassin because no one would believe she could do it. Juliette, on the other hand, was perpetually angry and sour, so maybe…

"What's funny?" Lauren asked. The child was standing in front of me.

"What?" My mind reeled backward. "Oh. It's a story on…" I looked down to see what I was reading. "…feathers."

Feathers? I was reading an article on feathers?

"DINNER!" Ned's voice bellowed from the dining room.

With a sigh, each of us got up and started out the door. I waited behind, just to make sure Caroline walked in front of me. She moved very slowly, making a big show out of putting a bookmark in the book, setting it on the table, and getting to her feet. She gave me a dirty look and then headed for the door. Once everyone was gone, I noticed that Dennis was still asleep.

"Dennis." I went over and prodded him. "Wake up. Dinner."

He didn't move. In fact, he was very still. I shook his shoulders, but the man didn't so much as bat an eyelash. Placing my fingers on the side of his neck, I couldn't find a pulse. I leaned down and put my head on his chest, but there was no thump of a heartbeat.

Dennis was dead.

CHAPTER FOURTEEN

How had this happened in front of us? He'd looked like he was asleep when Soo Jin and I came into the room. Was he, in fact, dead when we'd shown up? How was it managed? I pulled the afghan off the back of the couch and covered him up.

Then I walked down the hall to the dining room, bypassing that to go into the lounge. Only one statue and the action figure remained. The killer had time to kill Dennis in front of everyone, leave the room without being seen, and destroy another statue.

I was stunned and unsure how to play this with everyone else. I had to join the others, but what would I say? All kinds of ideas pummeled me as I made my way to the dining room. Guilt was one of them. I'd insisted that Caroline couldn't act if everyone was together. And I was wrong.

As I settled into my seat, the smell of pork chops had no effect on me. Sooner than later, people would notice Dennis wasn't here. Like it or not, I'd have to announce another murder.

Caroline's smug look as she was leaving was such a giveaway! Soo Jin was right. It was time to lock her up or tie her up.

Oddly enough, no one seemed to notice that Dennis wasn't with us. Either they'd given up worrying, or they thought he was still snoozing. In any event, they probably thought he was safe since the killer was one of us.

I didn't push it. Instead, I took a pork chop, scooped up some mashed potatoes, and ate in silence, like everyone else. Cautiously, I glanced around the table. No one looked up. They seemed to be fascinated by their own food. Maybe they didn't want to look up, thinking if they did, there'd be another dead body sitting across from them.

The girls were even quiet. They had a platter of chili cheese dogs and french fries that made me wonder if I could lure Miriam away to cook for me and Rex full time.

Unlike the others, the girls seemed introspective, as if each one was working through the case. That was when I noticed that Lauren had a bowl of Jell-O, and she was launching herself facedown into it, holding that position for a few seconds before coming up for air and doing it again. The girls studied her and made quiet comments. They were reenacting Thad's murder. I guess the gelatin made sense. They probably intuited that I'd never let them use the real thing.

Something got Betty's attention. She looked up and then studied everyone at the table. Her eyes grew wide on seeing Dennis's empty chair before resting on me. I shook my head, and she nodded. Then she went back to her supper. Good girl.

A large sheet cake was brought out, and as Miriam cut each piece, Ned handed it out. This seemed to cheer people up immensely, and there were even a few smiles around the table. And that was when it happened.

"Where's Dennis?" Caroline asked, her eyes narrowing, drilling into mine.

"Why don't you tell us, Dr. Regent?" I fired back.

She looked confused for a moment. Startled, even. "How would I know? You were the last one out of the room."

All eyes turned to me. It was time.

"Dennis is dead," I said simply.

I waited for the uproar, the questions, and angry accusations, but none came.

"Was he murdered?" Stacey squeaked. She was probably wondering how to tell his parents that their only child died at an event they were supposed to attend.

I shrugged. "I don't know. Dr. Body will have to take a look at him. In the meantime, I'd say it's time for bed." I pointed to the girls and indicated I wanted them to stay.

Everyone agreed, and there was a stampede up the stairs. The sounds of doors slamming were most likely followed by locks being turned.

Once everyone was gone, I looked around for Miriam and Ned. Who had disappeared. Again. In that case I helped myself to a huge piece of cake and a chili cheese dog.

"You're just going to sit there and eat?" Soo Jin asked.

"Yup. And when I'm good and done, we'll go to the conservatory. Until then, enjoy!"

The girls sat at the big table, each taking another slice of cake. Soo Jin threw her arms up in the air and joined us.

"What happened?" Soo Jin asked as she cut into the cake.

"He was the only one left in the room," I said. "I went to wake him up, but unfortunately, he was dead."

"Why didn't you tell anyone?" Betty's head cocked to one side. The question wasn't accusatory but full of curiosity.

"I figured it would be nice to eat without a murder, for a change. And I wanted to see who would be the first to say something."

Inez asked what was on everyone's mind. "Do you still think it's Caroline?"

I nodded. "She was the first one to ask. I'm guessing she wasn't getting the reaction she wanted. It galled her that she'd gone to the trouble of killing Dennis and no one noticed."

"And the figure?" Ava asked.

"Broken. There are only two left."

"And one is for you…" Lauren's voice trailed off.

"She'll go after Arthur, and maybe Violet again," Soo Jin said. "What do we do?"

I panicked. I ran up the stairs, two at a time, and knocked on Stacey's door. She answered immediately and agreed that she and Juliette would head to Arthur and Violet's room to watch them until I came back up.

When I returned, the girls and Soo Jin were in the conservatory examining the body.

She shook her head. "The poem said that this one sniffed some glue, which could mean poisoned. The easiest way to do that sneaking up on him would be injection, but there aren't any marks on him. He isn't showing any obvious signs of poison. In fact, he could've had a heart attack. It's hard to say."

I plopped into the chair where Caroline had been sitting. "Did you girls see Caroline move around the room when we were in the basement?"

Inez nodded. "She was over at the plant stand." The girl pointed to a huge metal shelving that held maybe a dozen plants. It was right next to Dennis's head.

"She looked at the plants and then returned to her chair." Lauren pointed at me. "But I think others wandered around the room a little. I can't really remember."

Betty spoke up. "We watched her. We watched everyone. She never touched him."

My vantage point, from Caroline's seat, had the perfect view of the deceased. But how did she do it?

"He certainly didn't sniff any glue," Lauren said.

"Sniffed glue!" I snapped my fingers and jumped to my feet. "What kind of aerosol poisons are there?"

Soo Jin thought about this for a moment. "Well, without my books from my office, I'm not sure. But it's possible that's how he was killed."

"This plant is dead!" Ava cried out. She was pointing to the plant closest to Dennis's head.

"So are those!" Inez pointed at the plants next to and below the first plant.

Soo Jin had the girls move out of the way. She bent down and looked at the dead plants.

"I think," she said at last, "that whatever the murderer used killed these plants. And it happened quickly."

I steeled myself. "That's it. It's time to deal with Caroline."

Five minutes later, I had Dr. Regent tied to a chair in the middle of her room, while Soo Jin and the girls carefully searched it. Stacey and Juliette stood in the doorway, watching. Arthur and Violet were locked up tight in their room.

"Don't touch anything," Soo Jin told the girls. "Don't open drawers or bottles. Just use your eyes."

"This is outrageous!" the constrained bowel doctor roared. "I'm suing all of you when this is over!"

Stacey's hands twisted with worry, but she didn't make a move to untie the bowel doctor.

"What did you use to kill Dennis?" I asked. "What aerosol was it? And if any of my girls get hurt, I'm going to kill you. Very slowly."

Caroline's mouth closed. She was done speaking.

After ten minutes of searching, Soo Jin called it off. "There's nothing here," she said.

"Untie me this minute!" Caroline roared.

I shook my head. "No way. You're staying here all night. It's for the safety of everyone else."

The doctor glared at me. "I'll scream all night until you let me go!"

I took a scarf from her closet and gagged her. She didn't like it, but I felt better.

"So," Soo Jin asked, "what now?"

Betty was checking the ropes to make sure the knots would hold. She gave me a thumbs-up.

"Now." I yawned. "Now we go to bed."

* * *

"Soo Jin! Will you stop pacing?" I said from my seat on the bed.

"Sorry!" she said, stopped, and came over to sit next to me.

The girls were out cold. Hearing that the killer was tied up probably was enough for them.

"I just don't know how she did it," she said for the tenth time.

"Killed Dennis?" I frowned. "Some sort of aerosol poison. I thought we'd decided."

She shook her head. "Not that. Enos. We know how everyone was killed except for Enos."

"I know. And it's bugging me." I picked at a piece of string. "We must be overlooking or forgetting something."

"Or it's not cyanide," Soo Jin said. "That's what has me going. Everything points to cyanide from his reddened skin and the smell of bitter almonds. But the speed at which it works throws a wrench into the works."

I shrugged. "It could have been in his food. We can't rule that out."

She shook her head. "You're right. It could have come from his fish. We just don't know for sure."

"In the end, this will be the sheriff's problem, not ours." And for once, I really, really wished the police were dealing with this. "At least our main suspect is tied up in her room."

"I wanted to believe that it was someone outside the group," she said. "Someone who was getting in, maybe hiding in the secret tunnel in the basement."

I thought about this. "That's plausible. We wouldn't even know someone else was here. It would make for the perfect murder."

It was a good theory—that Caroline could be the killer. Except for the murders of Enos and Dennis. Maybe we'd never know what her motives were there. Maybe she had done one bowel surgery too many and she snapped and decided to kill a houseful of people.

It happens more than you'd think. We had this guy at the Farm—the training facility for the CIA. Donny was great at everything, from jogging to interrogation to martial arts training. I was sure he was going to go on to a great career. He was the type of guy you'd expect to save the world.

The problem was, Don was losing it. And no one knew. Then one day, while we were qualifying on sniper rifles, something snapped. Don took off all of his clothes, ran to the commissary, where he smeared pickle relish all over himself, and declared that he was the King of Sweden.

People handle life differently. I could've lost it. When I was outed and lost the only job I'd ever had, I could've snapped and joined the circus or become a rutabaga farmer. But I didn't. I held it together.

Caroline wasn't holding it together.

* * *

A few hours later, Soo Jin and I passed out. When we woke up, it was daylight, and we were still wearing what we'd worn the day before.

"Look!" Lauren pointed out the window. "It's sunny!"

I ran to the window. She was right. The rain had stopped, and the sun was out. The boat was scheduled to come at one o'clock to pick us up, which was good because as Ned said, the radio had been destroyed, and our phones didn't work.

There was a spring in my step as I changed clothes and brushed my teeth. This was almost over! No one died during the night! We'd saved the day!

Well, not really. We'd have saved the day if we'd gotten to Caroline sooner. I felt very guilty about that.

"I guess we should check on our prisoner and see if she needs a bathroom break," I said brightly.

Soo Jin followed me to Caroline's door. I turned the handle and called out her name, before remembering that we'd gagged her. I opened the door and was confronted with something I certainly didn't expect.

Caroline's head lolled against the back of the chair, and she was completely limp. A piece of wire had been woven around her from neck to toe, and that wire was hooked up to a car battery. I'd seen this kind of thing before and was, in fact, too familiar with it.

Caroline had been electrocuted—CIA style.

CHAPTER FIFTEEN

A quick check showed that everyone else was fine. Arthur and Violet were still in their nightclothes and half asleep when we roused them to let us in. Stacey and Juliette were dressed when they answered the door.

No one was happy to hear the news.

We slouched down to the dining room together like a pack of disheartened zombies. Boxes of cereal, bowls and spoons, and a gallon of milk sat on the table. Ned and Miriam were nowhere to be found.

"You thought it was Dr. Regent!" Juliette snapped. Ah. There she was. Angry at me and ready to suspect the worst. I'd almost missed it.

I nodded. "I did. Apparently, I was wrong."

"Maybe she killed herself?" Arthur ventured. "She knew she was caught and knew she'd be in prison for the rest of her life and she committed suicide."

I shook my head. "She was still tied up. Someone added wire and the battery. It couldn't have been her."

"What about the statue?" Ava asked.

"It's probably broken," I said.

No one had any interest in seeing for themselves. I couldn't blame them.

My money was now on Ned and Miriam, but I was afraid to voice it. How did I get it so wrong about Caroline? "Roasted in the sun" from the poem referred to electrocution. I shivered. I'd basically gift wrapped the woman for the killer. How was I going to explain that?

And there was another problem. According to the poem, I was next. It would be pretty hard to nail the killer if they nailed me first.

We ate in silence. The break in the weather did little to raise our spirits. I didn't even have the energy to track Ned and Miriam down. If the goal was to break me, this killer was succeeding. I wasn't cut out for this—which was too bad, since we could really use a leader right now.

Even the girls seemed depressed. We were going to be rescued at one. It was nine. We had four hours left, and I was the only remaining victim listed in the poem.

"Now that the weather is good, when will the boat be here?" Violet asked.

"Not until one. We still don't have cell service or a working radio," I explained. "The boat is to come back here at one. Until then, we have to stay together."

Arthur spoke up. "What if the killer is on the outside? Someone we don't even know?"

Soo Jin said, "We've thought of that. That's why staying together is so important."

Stacey asked, "You mean someone else might be on the island with us?"

"It's possible." I didn't say that I wondered if it was Lana, because I wasn't sure.

The theory of an outside killer was something I didn't really want to consider because it would be much harder to solve. Either the killer was Arthur, Violet, Miriam, Ned, or an unknown entity. If it was a mysterious killer, how did they move around so we didn't see them? It had to be the tunnels, since four of the rooms had access to secret passages. For all we knew, Audrey Deivers had snapped and was living in the walls with Gertrude, picking us off one by one.

If we stayed in one of the rooms that didn't, we could avoid a sneak attack. That meant the conservatory, study, lounge, and kitchen were out. We could only use the billiard room, library, ballroom, and dining room.

The plan initially was for a farewell lunch before the guests left. We could stay in the dining room until lunch. But by the way people picked at their food, I was pretty sure all appetite was gone.

As I looked over the remaining guests, I wondered if they had the wherewithal to kill. They'd need strength and stealth. Ned was strong. Having worked for the Deivers, both he and Miriam probably knew about the underground passageways.

Should I confront them? Ned was much bigger than me, but I was pretty sure I could take him. Would it be best to get him alone? I wasn't sure that was possible. I'd never seen one without the other.

The room they always seemed to be in was the kitchen. There was no way I was going to deal with them in there. Too many knives. Should I do it in front of everyone? What if he lost it and attacked us all?

The killer was very careful to avoid being seen. Would Ned decide to chuck it and kill me anyway since I was the next on the list?

And what did I ever do to him or Miriam? Since the whole Caroline-Thad-Taylor-Wren love…um…square wasn't the reason, what were the motives for the other murders? Spree killers? They had a chance to fulfill some fantasy to take out innocent people? Sadly, that kind of thing happened.

What about Lana? She befriended Dennis and told him she was writing a book about me. I'd sworn I'd seen her a few months back in Who's There. Her motive? Probably pinning this on me. It would be sweet revenge to see me locked away in prison for the rest of my life.

It was a ridiculous thought. If I was the killer, what was my motive? I didn't know these people, and I certainly wouldn't hurt the Girl Scouts by killing off their biggest donors. How would Lana prepare a case against me? I'd been with Soo Jin almost the whole time.

I'd been the one who found the first broken figure in the lounge. I was a spy who knew how to poison and kill. There were other times when I'd run around the house alone, and I could've put myself at the end of the poem as a red herring. Would that be exploited? Had evidence been planted in my room? In my things?

Now I really wanted to search my stuff. But I couldn't leave any of these folks alone. Especially the girls. They'd been real troopers through all of this, probably due to their more morbid fascination with all things creepy. No, none of these people had it in them to hurt the kids. I truly believed that.

It had to be the staff or an outsider. I wasn't willing to bet the farm that it was Lana. It could be anyone—most likely someone I didn't even know. And I was next. How did the poem go? Something about going undercover in the CIA?

That didn't seem like a way to die, but I'd been oblivious to everything so far, so what did I know? If it were me, I wished they'd just take me out on the street instead of killing me and seven other people.

Miriam and Ned came in and cleared the plates. Violet asked if they had any playing cards. Miriam opened a drawer in the sideboard and handed her a pack. The elderly woman called the girls over and offered to teach them a game.

Good. I needed them to be distracted while I figured out what to do.

"What do you think?" Soo Jin asked. "You've been quiet a long time."

"I think our suspects are Ned, Miriam, Audrey Deivers, Gertrude, or someone outside, like Lana."

She rolled her eyes. "That really narrows it down."

"I think we keep the windows and doors shut. We wait out the next few hours here."

"Okay," Soo Jin said. She started to walk away but returned. "How do you think the killer will come for you?"

"I have no idea. I'm still not convinced they are going to let Violet out of here alive. They smashed her figurine. Whoever it was thought it was a done deal."

"Yes, but that's when we thought it was Caroline."

I thought about this and lowered my voice. "Do you think the killer is Arthur? That Violet was his endgame?"

We looked at the old man with new eyes. He was taller than his wife and sturdily built. After all, the man had been a hog farmer all of his life. Was it possible that he was the killer? Why would he kill his wife? Okay, I'd watched enough episodes of *Forensic Files* to know that the most common killer of a woman was her husband.

The idea gained traction in my brain. Was cyanide used on farms? He could've poisoned Enos's food or injected him with the cyanide. No one mentioned where he was when Taylor slipped away. He was certainly strong enough to kill her and

Thad. And his room was right next to Caroline's. Wren could've been easily convinced to try on Taylor's dress—she wouldn't suspect a sweet old man.

Suddenly, I didn't want him anywhere near the girls or Violet. But how to get him away without making him suspicious? I could send him to the kitchen and follow him. But that would just provide him with an opportunity to work his plan alone.

I closed my eyes and took a couple of deep breaths. I was going mad from all of this. My mind was racing, making me a mess. I was terrified of everything that my overactive imagination could think of.

"Are you alright, dear?" Violet asked.

Every set of eyes was on me. I had everyone's attention…Wait! That was an idea! Draw the killer off! Force his hand! And do it away from everyone else in hopes that I'd survive it.

"I'm fine." I waved her off. "It's just a headache. I'm going to run upstairs to get some aspirin."

The old woman looked startled. "Do you think that's wise? Someone should go with you."

Hoping I was acting as if I hadn't a care in the world, I replied, "I'll be alright. I can take care of myself. Would you make sure to watch the girls for a minute?"

She smiled broadly. "Of course!"

Soo Jin slid over to me. "What are you doing?"

I shrugged. "Nothing."

"You're setting yourself up as bait, aren't you?" She folded her arms over her chest.

"Maybe," I said slowly. "Just stay here. I'll be back."

"Merry," she warned. "This is a terrible idea."

"If something happens to me, you have to take my place in the troop." I winked at her.

Soo Jin blocked the doorway. I gently shoved her aside. "I'm doing this. Stay here. You can watch me go upstairs. Then watch to see if anyone follows me. Okay?" I fled before she could stop me.

Yes, this was a stupid idea. Believe me—it wasn't the first time I'd done that. While stupid ideas often led to death, they also led to clues. I was rooting for the latter.

Once upstairs, I headed straight to Arthur and Violet's room. Hopefully, I had enough time to search for whatever I was looking for. Closing the door quietly behind me, I looked around.

I'd been in here only once, to put out the envelopes for the game. I couldn't recall that anything was different from the other rooms, but I was wrong. This was the master suite. The Deivers' bedroom. The furniture was expensive and the decorating first rate. It made perfect sense that the Kasinskis were put in here. They'd been donating to the Girl Scouts for years, according to Stacey.

The bed was made. Clothes were neatly folded in the suitcase or hanging on the back of the door. A lovely painting of the house and island hung on the wall. I stepped closer to examine it. It was an idyllic setting with children playing in the yard. It was sad to think that this house was tarnished by murder.

"What are you doing?" Betty's voice at my elbow made me leap into the air, landing in a defensive crouch.

I looked at the door. Still closed.

"What are you doing here? How did you get in? Why aren't you with the others?" My rapid-fire questions matched my heartbeat. I didn't want to draw out the killer with her in here.

She shrugged, as if she snuck up on me like this every day. To be fair, she kind of did.

"I wanted to make sure you were okay." She smiled. "I made this." The girl handed me a large dagger taped to the end of a pool cue. That was sweet.

"Why did you slip away? They'll notice!" The last thing I wanted was for everyone to find me snooping.

"Lauren and I asked to use the bathroom. Lauren's still there, ready to tell the others that we're still busy."

"How did you get into this room?"

She grinned. "The basement doesn't have the only hidden passages in this house." She led me to the closet and opened the door. The clothes were parted in the middle, and a small door was open in the back.

"What? When? How?" I sputtered.

"We found it this morning around five. You were still sleeping, so we decided to check Thad's crime scene. This goes up into the attic and comes down into his room."

"Is it the only one?" I turned on my cell's flashlight app and aimed it into the darkness.

"It also goes into Taylor's room. I meant to tell you. I guess we forgot."

"Show me," I insisted as I dove into the closet.

Betty closed the closet door behind us, took my cell out of my hand, and found a light switch just inside the passageway. Lights went on, and we climbed a steep and narrow staircase that opened into an attic. The place was covered in dust everywhere, but there was a clean trail that went over to the opposite corner. No footprints, just the floor.

I followed her to that corner, and we went down another set of stairs, coming out in Thad and Wren's closet. Then we crossed the room where a large mirror was hanging on the wall. Betty yanked on one side, and it swung open like a door. We went through that and emerged in Taylor's closet.

I sat down on the bed. Of course my troop found this. They were smart, inventive girls who didn't stay put even when ordered to. The connection between Arthur's and Thad's room made it clear that he could've easily slipped into the room, bludgeoned, and suffocated Thad before slipping into the closet and reappearing in his room.

He could have done this with Violet in the bathroom. Caroline's room was next door to theirs. He could've killed her while his wife was sleeping. We left the room, crossed the hall, and went back into the Kasinskis' room. Was Arthur the killer? It sure seemed like it. At least for Thad's and Caroline's deaths. But he wasn't anywhere near Enos at lunch, and I couldn't remember if he'd been upstairs when Wren was pushed.

"Did you know…" Betty tapped me on the arm. "That the killings have been done boy-girl-boy-girl? Well, until yours, that is."

"I guess I didn't," I admitted.

"That's weird," Betty said. "That's how we were seated for that first lunch too."

Something went *ping* in my brain. And then I spotted a book on the dresser. I'd seen that book before. Walking over, I picked it up. *The Canterbury Tales*. Thad had been reading that. I raced out the door and into Thad's room. What I saw pulled everything together.

I knew who the killer was. I knew why they'd killed. I still didn't have all of the *hows*, but it didn't matter.

"Come on!" I shouted to Betty, and we ran down the stairs and into the dining room.

CHAPTER SIXTEEN

Soo Jin's eyes widened. "Betty? Where's Lauren?" She got up as if to head to find her, but I waved her to sit back down.

"Go get your partner in crime," I said to the girl.

As she dashed out of the room, Soo Jin stood up. "It's not safe!"

I shook my head and set the book down on the sideboard behind me. "It's perfectly safe."

"But the killer…" Stacey started.

"Is in this room. So I'm not worried."

Lauren and Betty joined us and sat down, just as Miriam and Ned appeared with coffee. I asked them to take their seats.

"You really had me going." I started to pace but made eye contact with no one in particular. "I was so sure about everything. Thought I knew what was going on. But I didn't."

Soo Jin pressed, "Cut to the chase, please."

I ignored her. "This whole time I was wrapped up in that 'Eight Little Girl Scouts' poem. But this wasn't about that at all. That was something to throw us off track." I picked up the book and opened it. One corner was torn out. Pulling the corner from my pocket, I was able to repair it.

"What's that?" Stacey asked.

"It's *The Canterbury Tales*. And it seems to be the most popular book in the house. I've found it connected to a few of the victims and the killer. This wasn't about the poem or the murder mystery game. This was about punishment."

"What are you talking about?" Soo Jin asked.

I ignored her question and continued. "I hated having to read this book in college. But sometimes the books you dislike stick with you more than the books you like. And there was one theme that I never forgot. The theme that ran through the whole book. About the seven deadly sins."

I held up my hand and ticked them off. "Gluttony, greed, lust, envy, sloth, pride, and Wrath. That's me. Wrath." I kind of liked how I'd been plugged into this. I didn't tell them that.

"I don't understand," Juliette said.

"The victims here were killed for committing one of the seven deadly sins. Enos was an overweight slob who was killed while eating. He's gluttony. Taylor's obsession at being the first and best—which was why she was killed with a trophy and for stealing another woman's husband, was about greed."

"Thad was lust because he was having an affair with Taylor!" Soo Jin cried out.

"What about envy?" Ava asked.

I nodded. "Wren was envy. She envied Taylor—which was why she was murdered wearing the dead woman's dress."

"Dennis was lazy—that's why sloth!" Stacey added.

Everyone seemed pleased that they were connecting pieces of the puzzle. In a weird way, we were playing a game. Only this one had real dead bodies.

Inez frowned. "But Violet and Caroline were both targets, and there's only one left—pride."

I nodded. "We were right in thinking that one of the guests was the killer and that only seven were the real targets. Pride was the last sin. The remaining punishment. Which meant that the other attempt was a red herring."

I turned to face Kevin the Killer. "Isn't that right, Violet?"

A gasp of shock went around the table, but the old woman was beaming from ear to ear next to her shocked husband.

"You got it! Caroline was pride—because she was so arrogant and thought nobody else was as good as she was."

"You never intended to kill me," I asked, "did you?"

"Oh no, dear! I'd hoped to match wits with you, and you did very well!"

Soo Jin's and everyone else's mouths dropped open. "Mrs. Kasinski is the killer?"

Violet and I nodded in sync. "That's right," I added.

Stacey jumped to her feet. "But why? Why kill these people?"

The old woman waved at her to sit back down. "I know this was a terrible imposition on your hospitality, and to make up for murdering your donors, I want you to know that I'm leaving everything to the Girl Scouts in my will."

Stacey and Juliette were stunned.

"I know the surface motives," I said. "But I don't know why you did it. What made you decide to kill?"

Violet took a sip of tea then slowly and gingerly got to her feet. "I never wanted to get married early and live out my years on a hog farm. I wanted to have an exciting life filled with adventure and danger. Like you! But my parents never liked that idea. So two weeks after graduating from high school, I did what they wanted, married Arthur, and spent my entire life resenting it."

"What?" Arthur gasped.

"Arthur, please shut up," Violet said gently. When he did, she continued. "As the years went on and I slopped hogs, balanced ledgers, attended Pork Producer meetings, and ruled over the Porkettes, I'm sad to say I became angrier and angrier at what I'd lost."

"But I…" her husband started.

"Arthur, I don't want to have to tell you again. Interrupting others is rude. Don't make me stab you with this butter knife."

Arthur slid his chair and himself out of her reach but said nothing.

She turned a beaming face back to the rest of us. "When I heard about you in the papers, being exposed by that horrid vice president, I felt sorry for you. As a major contributor to your father's campaigns, I recognized you. You look just like your grandmother, Adelaide Wrath, by the way."

"Um…thank you?" It kind of seemed like a compliment that she went on this killing spree to impress me.

"That's what started the whole ball rolling," Violet continued. "My father was a judge. And a good one. I was too old to become a spy, but I could become a judge."

"You sentenced all these people and carried out those sentences!" Soo Jin chastised.

The girls nodded approvingly…to Violet. I'd have to work on that.

"Yes. I did. I know it was wrong, but for once in my life, I was doing something exciting. Something no one thought I was capable of."

"Why didn't you kill Mr. Kasinski?" Betty raised her hand. She was asking out of curiosity, which seemed a tad disturbing.

"That's an excellent question, young lady!" Violet clapped her hands together. "You girls are amazing. I hope you do what you want to do when you grow up and don't follow my path."

"Hey!" Arthur said weakly as he scooted a few more inches away.

"I didn't kill my husband because I wanted him to see what I was capable of." She cocked her head to one side. "Although I did toy with it."

Her husband turned an alarming shade of red.

Violet ignored him. "I grew up running around this island. My aunt once owned it. I know every inch. Including where the secret passages are." She winked at the girls. "So it was easy for me to slip in and out of rooms."

"There are secret passages?" Juliette's jaw dropped.

I interrupted to briefly explain before giving Violet the floor once again.

"It was my idea," she continued, "to have the Mystery Night here on this island. I've known the Deivers for years, and Audrey promised to pretend it was her idea, just for fun. And then I made my guest list. Dennis's parents were always buying tickets to events they couldn't attend. I'd convinced them to make their lazy son go in their stead.

"When I ran into Taylor at an event, I appealed to her Girl Scout background. She couldn't wait to have a roomful of people to lord her achievements over. It was all too easy. And when I ran into Caroline, I just mentioned that this would be a good opportunity to show Taylor how successful she'd become."

"How did you get the Gables on board?" Stacey asked. "I wasn't sure they were going to come."

Violet laughed sweetly. "I knew about Thad and Taylor's affair—everyone did. I once again ran into Wren at an event and suggested that this might offer a romantic getaway with her husband. I didn't mention that Taylor would be there." She started to stare off into the distance. "I'll admit—that felt a bit mean."

"What about Enos?" I nudged. She was on a roll, and I didn't want to interrupt things by saying it was more than a bit mean to invite people here and then kill them off one by one. If there's anything I'd learned from Disney movies—you have to keep the villain monologuing.

She turned to face me, wearing a mask of confusion. "Enos?" Then her eyes focused. "Oh! Him! That young man was awful. He created one silly invention then did nothing after that. He didn't have to work as hard as Arthur and I did for our wealth. He could've changed the world with his fortunes, but he didn't. He just got fat and became bored. I sent him an invite, hoping he'd come just for the novelty of it, and he did."

"How did you kill him?" I asked. "Miriam told me we were supposed to have lasagna instead of fish, but the menu changed."

Stacey blanched. "Mrs. Kasinski asked if we could substitute fish for lunch. I had no idea that was so she could poison it."

Violet nodded. "Sleight of hand, my dear. As I had reached across him to get the salt, I dropped the powder onto his fish. He might have tasted it in pasta, but the fish would disguise it." She looked at me for approval. I wasn't sure what to think about that.

"And slipping away to kill Taylor?" Soo Jin asked.

"That was easy. You were all so engrossed in finding that rabbit that you didn't notice I'd been gone."

"You used the secret passage through the attic to kill Thad," I added.

"Yes! Good job! The stairs are so hard on my knees these days, but yes, that's how I did it. As for Caroline, I waited for Arthur to fall asleep and slipped next door. I'd hidden the equipment in her closet earlier that day. Since you'd tied her to a chair, it was so easy to electrocute her."

"What about Wren?" I asked quickly, wishing I could forget that I'd handed Caroline over to her killer so easily.

She looked confused. "What about her, dear?"

"Thad's wife, Wren? You dressed her in Taylor's clothes and pushed her down the stairs."

The old lady chuckled softly. "Oh, right. I did do that. But I didn't dress her. It was easy to convince her to try it on. I just told her that she'd look much better in it than Taylor did."

I thought about this. "Weren't you in the library with Arthur?"

She nodded. "He fell asleep. Like he always does. I hurried down the stairs as Wren fell. Granted, with these knees it took a little longer than I'd hoped, but no one noticed a thing."

Soo Jin cleared her throat. "And Dennis?"

Violet grinned widely. "It was a special poison disbursed through aerosol. I made it myself. Tested it on rats in the barn. There are three kinds of toxins in it—I can't remember the exact formula. My first invention! Isn't that grand?"

"How did you do the branch?" Betty asked.

Violet winked at the girl. "You girls are so smart! I really wish I could be a leader. There's a lot I could teach you!"

Yeah, like how to kill a houseful of people. That was the kind of leadership we didn't need.

"She ran a wire from the porch to the tree," Lauren nodded matter-of-factly. "My guess is the branch was cut almost all the way."

"That's right!" Violet clapped her hands.

"But you were under the branch when it broke." Inez tilted her head to one side.

"I rigged it so that one tug would be enough to force the branch to break the rest of the way," our killer said. "That was the hardest one because I had to time it just right to get close to the tree before the branch dropped. I had to practice on the farm for about three months until I got it right," She turned to her husband. "Remember, Arthur, when you complained about all those branches being down in the south field?"

Arthur gulped loudly.

His wife beamed at us, as if waiting for applause. In her mind, she'd pulled off the crime of the century. Actually, I had to agree with that. Violet Kasinski was diabolical. She would've made an amazing spy. Too bad she didn't join the CIA before launching a geriatric killing spree at my Girl Scout event.

The woman started to frown. She looked sad.

"I can't believe you managed all that." I gushed a little. "I know career spies who couldn't have pulled that off."

That seemed to be what she wanted to hear, and she beamed, nudging Arthur as if to show him what she was made of. Arthur was looking a little green around the gills, and I wondered if she had poisoned him so he would die after her fiendish diatribe.

"I'm sorry," I said after a moment. "But I'll have to ask you to sit down and stay there until we can get you to the authorities."

She did. "I'm so excited that I was able to do it! I really wanted to impress you! When Stacey mentioned that you'd be part of the show, I thought this was a great opportunity!"

Stacey went pale. "You're right. You did ask me if Merry was coming. I totally forgot."

I was worried that the younger woman would have a stroke after finding out she'd been manipulated into getting these victims here. I felt badly for her. I made a mental note to make a large donation to the camp program when this was all over.

I'd be lying if I said I wasn't flattered. No one had ever killed anyone to impress me before. Well, that wasn't totally true. Once in Peru, a Paraguayan spy (a short-order cook who doubled as the prime minister's private secretary) took out a rabid llama that was racing toward me. I'm not sure that was the same thing.

Still, I wasn't sure Violet had thought this through. Now that she was a murderer, did she think she'd just go home?

"But you're going to prison," I said. "You have lost your freedom. You'll never be able to go anywhere you want or do what you want to do."

The woman smiled warmly. "I'm already in a prison, dear. But it's nice of you to worry about me."

"Do you mean your marriage? Or living on the farm?" I asked. "Because you won't be going back there."

Violet shook her head. "The farm has been my prison since I was seventeen. I'm not going to comment on my marriage because it makes me too upset and want to kill Arthur here."

Arthur fainted.

"But that's not what I'm talking about. I'm referring to my disease. I have Alzheimer's."

For a moment I wondered if that would get her off by reason of insanity.

Violet sighed. "I'll probably be sent to a correctional facility that has memory care. Soon, I won't even know that this happened. I won't know who I am or where I am. That's the saddest part."

For a moment, I felt a wave of sympathy for the woman. She grew up in a different time. I had freedoms she couldn't even imagine. If I'd married right out of high school and stayed in Iowa, never travelled or got an education, would I have done the same thing? Okay, the answer to that is no. I wouldn't have killed six people to make a point. Two, yes. Three…maybe. But six? That was overkill in my book.

I thought about what she'd said. Rex and I had met after my career was over. I had something for myself before sharing it with someone else. Sure, we'd only been married a couple of months, but we'd been together a few years.

I knew who I was, or at least, I thought I did, before I met him. It seemed unfathomable to share a life with someone before seeing what I could do. When she thought she'd lived her whole life in a prison, I knew she meant her marriage at an early age.

But that didn't make killing all these people right. It didn't matter how arrogant or awful they were, and unless they were Hitler or Stalin (and in some cases, Bernie Madoff), they couldn't be judged and sentenced to death by her. Thad and Taylor were dreadful. Caroline was arrogant. Wren was weak. Enos devoured one empty experience after another. Dennis, on the other hand, did absolutely nothing.

That did not give Violet the right to sentence them to death. People changed. And they should've had the opportunity to do that. Even if they never did.

It opened my eyes to my future. I loved working with the girls. I loved making a life with Rex. But maybe it was time to look at doing more. Maybe it was time to find a job or something else that would make my life move forward.

And maybe the first step was to find out once and for all if Lana was really here, tormenting me on the edges of my life. Whether she was really writing a book about me, or involved in local murders, it was time to find her and deal with her once and for all.

CHAPTER SEVENTEEN

Ned kept an eye on Violet, who smiled sweetly at him and assured us all that her killing spree was over, while Soo Jin and I went to the dock to wait for the boat. The weather had cleared, and a large, bright rainbow was emblazoned from one end of the lake to the other.

"I can't believe that," Soo Jin murmured. "Violet's life drove her to kill half a dozen people. And here I thought she had it all together."

"Why's that?"

"Well." She shrugged. "I've always wanted what you have. What she had. A relationship that would lead to spending the rest of my life with my soul mate."

My jaw dropped open. "Are you serious? You have an amazing life!"

She stared at me as if I'd grown two heads. "I'm a medical examiner who lives in a small town in Iowa."

"Yes." I nodded. "But you have a lot of work."

"The bodies do tend to pile up," she agreed. "And that's interesting and all. But I'd like something a little more spiritual."

"You aren't planning on leaving us, are you?" We were just becoming friends. I couldn't have made it through this weekend without the Korean–American knockout.

"Merry." She turned to face me. "You were a spy! You travelled all over the world! You went on adventures! I came here after medical school. In Chicago. Not interesting at all."

Man! I couldn't believe that this wonder woman envied me! She was smart and beautiful and talented. I looked like I'd just crawled out of bed, wearing clothes that I'd slept in. Not just this morning—every day! How could she possibly envy me?

"And no," she added with a small smile, "I'm not planning on leaving. I love Who's There. I adore you, and the girls, and Kelly, and Rex and Riley."

We stood on the dock, looking toward the horizon. A boat motor hummed in the distance. The sound of people running up behind us made me spin and adjust into a defensive stance, but once I saw it was the girls, I relaxed. Lauren was holding and petting a very nervous Gertrude. I wondered if she wasn't used to being outside.

"What are you doing out here?" I asked.

Betty shrugged. "It's boring in there."

I looked at her. "Boring? You were hanging out with a murderer. How is that boring?"

Lauren piped up, "She admitted what she used to poison Enos, but she wouldn't tell us where she got the cyanide and lubricant."

I bit my lip, but Soo Jin burst out laughing.

The girls looked at each other then back at me.

"Don't worry about that." I put my arms around Ava and Inez. "Let the police figure that out."

On the horizon we spotted the boat that was coming toward us. I could just make out Kelly and Linda waving at us. Boy, were they going to be sad they'd missed this.

"And"—I bent down to their level—"let's keep the thing about the lubricant between us, okay?" The last thing I needed was for Kelly to have a heart attack.

We waited in silence as the boat drew near and eventually pulled up to the dock. I explained what was going on to the captain, who immediately called the sheriff's office on his radio. Kelly and Linda looked suitably horrified as the girls told them about each grisly murder.

"Seriously!" Kelly chastised me. "I can't leave you alone for one weekend!"

I waved my hands in front of me defensively. "I didn't do it! I had nothing to do with it!"

Soo Jin asked the captain to have the sheriff call my husband, Rex, and he did so. Within an hour and a half, the dock had three boats, four EMTs, Sheriff Carnack and three deputies, and my husband, Detective Rex Ferguson, giving me a look I was all too familiar with.

They took Violet away, along with a very shaken and disturbed Arthur. Stacey and Juliette gave their statements and said they'd wait to explain things to the Deivers. Once we'd collected our luggage and taken the boat back to shore, Soo Jin and the girls went with Kelly and Linda, while I climbed into Rex's SUV.

On the drive home, I stared at the farms that dotted the scenery.

"Are you okay?" Rex said finally.

I nodded. "Just promise me one thing."

"That you can have Pizza Rolls when we get home?"

"Okay, two things." I loved Pizza Rolls. "Promise me that our life together won't be so dull that I want to kill a houseful of people."

"Merry." He slid his hand over mine. "I can promise you that life with you will never, ever be dull. No matter how much I want that."

I let out a deep breath and settled back into the seat. I thought about Riley's work as a private investigator and how he had an open invitation for me to join him as a PI. Maybe I should take him up on it.

I didn't tell Rex about Lana. I didn't know if she was real or some sort of red herring. But one thing was for sure. I was going to find out.

* * *

The next day, Riley called his old contacts at the CIA to alert them to the possibility of Lana being in the area and trying to write a tell-all book. I wasn't sure they believed it, but Riley and I had already decided to look into it on our own. If Lana was in Central Iowa, we were going to find her. Maybe I could take a page out of Violet's playbook and make sure Lana was never found again? Would that be too much?

The Deivers were not happy about the multiple murders committed in their home, but they didn't blame the Girl Scouts.

A few weeks after the cursed Mystery Night, I heard from Stacey that with all the media attention and curiosity seekers, the Deivers had decided to open up the house for Mystery Night weekends complete with séances to contact the ghosts of the victims. Gertrude could help, as the sound of her scurrying around inside the walls would fool folks into believing there were ghosts around. From what I understood, they were booked two years out already.

Betty and the girls found out what the lubricant that smothered Thad was really for. The next two meetings were rendered useless by the giggling hysteria that broke out. Kelly insisted right to the bitter end that the lube was for car axles. The girls didn't believe it for one minute. Smart girls.

Linda was surprised that her innocent cozy mystery night went the way it did, but she kept it all in perspective and even agreed to consider writing another one for the Girl Scouts. This time, instead of donors, it would be a dinner party with actors playing the parts. And as long as there weren't any problems with the actors, I was fairly certain no one would be killed for real.

During the ensuing investigation, Soo Jin met the super handsome prosecuting attorney handling the case. They hit it off and have been dating ever since. His name was Eduardo Ruiz, and he seemed like a great guy. But if he so much as looks at her funny, I'm going all Violet on him.

That's right—*Violet* became a term people used as a euphemism for murder. In a way, she kind of became a sort of folk hero. She was interviewed in all the major magazines and TV news channels. The woman balanced her killing spree with a softening attitude toward the victims, who became known as the Kasinski Six.

Arthur went back to his farm and stayed there. He refused to give interviews, and eventually the media got bored and went away. I'd heard rumors that he was going to move to the Pacific Northwest to live with his brother, but I had no idea if that was true. I felt a little sorry for him, but not too much. How did he not know his wife was so unhappy? I was pretty sure that Rex would know immediately if I even hinted at a murderous rage.

Of all the victims, Dennis Blunt's parents were the only family members who did something truly amazing. They'd set up a scholarship in his honor and made gifts in his name to the Girl Scouts, the Boys and Girls Club, and a bizarre cat charity I'd never heard of. It was the most good Dennis had ever done in his life…and ironically, it was in his death.

Miriam and Ned left Penny Island shortly after the police finished interviewing them. They moved across the state and opened a small café in Dubuque, where the specialty was lasagna. It was a popular place, and I wasn't ashamed to admit that I'd ordered lasagna shipped to my house from their place. Twice.

Stacey went back to the Council and offered to resign, feeling that this was somehow her fault. Instead, they promoted her for keeping her head during all of this, and she now toured councils all over the country, giving lectures on how to keep it together when a little old lady kills off all your donors.

Juliette was the strangest development in that she seemed to drop her blazing hatred for me. For weeks afterward, there were no attacks on my qualifications as a leader, no pulling of our paperwork to harass us for the smallest thing. And I heard a rumor that she actually praised me for solving the case and keeping our girls safe.

Betty and Lauren learned how to make a pipe bomb, which they detonated at a meeting. Instead of nails and bits of metal, they'd filled it with candy and gum. Kelly's fury eventually died down, but I was still forced to begin every meeting with, "We aren't going to make any more weapons, right?" I get the feeling that Kelly thinks this speech somehow falls short of her expectations.

My pets didn't seem to notice I'd even been gone. Rex reported that Philby had gotten into the fridge and "liberated" an entire salmon, eating the entire thing in twenty minutes, and then vomited for two days, while Martini took naps in the bathtub for hours at a time. And while Leonard was still a little afraid of Philby, he wasn't cowering in fear of her anymore when she strutted around wearing a rubber werewolf mask.

* * *

Violet Kasinski held her own through a long trial. People came from miles around to wait in line for a chance of sitting in the courtroom. I was there as a witness, as was Soo Jin. But what we said wasn't as fascinating to the public as Violet's own words regarding her life on the farm. It was kind of like *Little House on the Prairie*—if Laura Ingalls Wilder snapped and went on a killing spree, instead of becoming a beloved children's author.

Violet basked in the glow of the attention for the ten-day trial. And when the jury declared her "guilty," she looked happier than I'd ever seen her. As the judge pronounced a sentence that included life in prison at a facility with memory care, Violet pumped her fist in the air and yelled, "Crackin!"

A couple of weeks into her stay in prison, we found out that she'd started a gang of ladies who knitted shiv cozies in the afternoons and spent every evening trying to remember where they'd put their needles. They became quite intimidating to the other inmates, often illegally selling yarn and cigarettes inside on the black market. They called Violet, "Violent Vi," much to her joyous approval. My troop even visited from time to time, although we had to be careful now that we discovered Betty was smuggling in hard candy.

In a strange way, I was happy for Violet. Oh sure, I would've preferred that she hadn't killed anyone. But it seemed to me that in that one moment, she'd felt like she'd made up for a life lost on the farm. Running a prison gang seemed like an added perk.

* * *

Weeks after the trial, as Rex and I settled on the couch one night with popcorn and a movie, I realized that even though my life was quieter now (with the exception of someone dropping dead around me on a regular basis), I couldn't complain. I had a balance that Violet didn't have, somewhere between the outrageous and the mundane. I'd been pining for my old career for the last few years. But that was just silly. I had adventure with my troop…with the mysteries that seemed to follow me everywhere…with my new and improved friendship with Soo Jin…with my boring date nights with my new husband.

As Philby slapped a piece of popcorn out of my hand, hunted and ate it, as Martini walked across the couch and fell over asleep midway between us, as Leonard climbed onto Rex's lap without withering under Philby's evil gaze, I knew that I had everything I ever needed to live a happy and contented life.

Especially knowing that at any moment there would be another mystery just around the corner. And that sounded perfect to me.

ABOUT THE AUTHOR

Leslie Langtry is the *USA Today* bestselling author of the *Greatest Hits Mysteries* series, *Sex, Lies, & Family Vacations*, *The Hanging Tree Tales* as Max Deimos, the *Merry Wrath Mysteries,* the *Aloha Lagoon Mysteries,* and several books she hasn't finished yet, because she's very lazy.

Leslie loves puppies and cake (but she will not share her cake with puppies) and thinks praying mantids make everything better. She lives with her family and assorted animals in the Midwest, where she is currently working on her next book and trying to learn to play the ukulele.

To learn more about Leslie, visit her online at:
http://www.leslielangtry.com

Enjoyed this book? Check out these other reads available now from Leslie Langtry:

www.GemmaHallidayPublishing.com

CPSIA information can be obtained
at www.ICGtesting.com
Printed in the USA
LVHW112050180922
728694LV00004B/458

Bootleggers, Bottles & Badges